Rupert Lally

Solid State Memories

Cover illustration by

Hannes Pasqualini

This paperback second edition published 2022
Text ©2017 Rupert Lally
Illustration ©2017 Hannes Pasqualini

ISBN: 9798826940877
Imprint: Independently published

For my Family

Solid

State

Memories

ALSO BY RUPERT LALLY:

Backwater

Contents

Foreword

We've all heard the old adage of not judging a book by its cover, but what about creating a book because of its cover? The book you're currently holding is an example of the latter.

When my friend Hannes Pasqualini offered to create a cover for a forthcoming project as a 40th birthday present to me, I knew I had to make something special in order to do justice to what I knew would be a wonderful piece of artwork. I'd been a fan of Hannes' work for several years, particularly the covers he'd drawn for the manuals of the various Hex Inverter eurorack modular synthesiser modules, which had reminded me a little of the 80s Marvel comics I'd grown up with.

I'd been trying to push myself to do more writing since my father's death in 2014, so this seemed a good opportunity to attempt something longer than the short fiction I'd written previously. Setting myself a rough deadline of 3-4 months I started writing, adapting an idea I'd first had a decade previously into something more suitable to accompany the electronic soundtrack that I knew I would also be making. Whilst most of the original idea, which had been a Le Carré-esque tale of someone slowly discovering that their long term partner, who has gone missing, is an MI:5 agent, was jettisoned; I was able to keep the initial idea of the protagonist waking to find their partner missing as well as much of the dialogue between Alex (who was originally written as a man) and Rachel when they first meet.

The rest of the plot only really began to coalesce after a conversation with my friend Colin Hussey, who'd recently seen a documentary about memory on You Tube. After watching the same documentary myself, it became clear that it could provide the background to this new version of the story and I was able to incorporate many of the key figures that were interviewed in the section detailing the history of the scientific study of memory.

Finally, once the manuscript was nearly ready, I was very fortunate to have my old school friend and now writer and proof reader, Stephen Ball, look it over and offer his feedback.

Eventually, both the novella and album were finished and released into the world but as with all good stories that wasn't quite the end. I subsequently felt that simply including the novella as a PDF alongside the album download meant that it was often slightly overlooked. When Nick Langley at Third Kind Records, who loved the album, suggested a remastered vinyl release, then it seemed clear to me that it was high time that the novella came out from behind the album's shadow and stood on its own two feet. Writer Alistair Owen, who I'd befriended on Twitter after he'd read some of my film blog posts, encouraged me to make the novella available on Kindle - something he'd done himself, a few years previously. Having gone that far, it made sense to finally produce a physical version as well (something I'd had in mind since the beginning, but hadn't gotten around to) and the result is what you now hold in your hands and I would like to also thank Chris Lambert for his invaluable advice about self-publishing.

Despite its short length, this novella remains something I'm very proud of. It demonstrated that I was capable of writing something longer than a short story and provided an important stepping stone in my evolution as a writer. Without it, I wouldn't have dared attempt the full length novel I'm currently in the process of finishing or perhaps have had the courage to include short fiction alongside a number of my subsequent music releases. Most of all, the favourable response it gathered from those who read it helped convince me that I should continue to write in those inevitable moments when, like many writers, I begin to doubt that I have created anything that's worth reading.

Rupert Lally
2021

1

The best lie is the one the liar, themselves, believes.

I woke up without you.

Later, I would become convinced that I already knew this before I opened my eyes, but whether I really thought that at the time, I can't say. Lying there, with the light streaming in through the blinds was when I first noticed that your head wasn't on the pillow next to me. Judging by the pristine condition of your side of the bed you hadn't been there the whole night long.

Where were you?

I rolled over and swung my legs out of the bed. My head hurt as I sat upright. A dull, persistent pain from the base of my neck, like muscle stiffness only more acute. I walked over to the window. It was past 9, already.

I went next door to the bathroom and splashed some cold water on my face. That's when I noticed the plaster in the crook of my elbow. A small plaster, like the type they give you at the doctor's when you've had an injection. I peeled the plaster away and sure enough,

5

there was the tell-tale dot and small yellow bruise of a recent needle mark.

When had this happened?

I had no memory of going to the doctor whatsoever. In fact, the last time I remembered being at the doctor's at all was 6 months ago, when I needed a new prescription for my Asthma medicine and even then I'd only seen the receptionist. I went back to the bedroom, threw on some clothes and headed downstairs to the lab.

Like a great many people, I lived where I worked. The almost complete depletion of fossil fuels, decline of the economy, a series of global pandemics and the steady rise of both automation processes and connectivity eventually reversed the trend of the Industrial Revolution. Cities shrank instead of growing as, little by little, factories and shops closed and the inner city areas were reclaimed to provide housing for a workforce of shut-ins.

Aside from one bar, two coffee shops and a deli, my entire neighbourhood which had once been a thriving industrial area full of factories and offices, was now totally residential. Why bother to commute to work when you can do it all from your portable device at home? Why go out and shop when everything can be delivered to your door, within a matter of hours, from one of the many fully automated warehouses somewhere on the outskirts of the city? Now that hardly anyone commuted, the roads were largely clear and deliveries were, therefore, much faster. Aside from you, weeks had often gone by without my seeing or conversing with anyone else other than some delivery people and Phil, my lab assistant.

When I walked down the wrought iron spiral staircase that led from my living quarters to the lab below Phil was already there working. He looked up as I hit the second to last step.

"Hey," he said, only half taking his eyes off of the microscope in front of him, "late night?"

"Hmmm...yeah, I guess..." My throat felt dry. I headed over to the refrigerator and grabbed a bottle of water from it.

Phil had been my lab assistant for close to three years. He had taken over from Joanne, who had been such a rising star in her chosen field of microbiology that it came as little surprise when after just 4 months she announced she'd been headhunted by a large pharmaceutical company to head up a new project. Phil was the opposite to Jo. It wasn't that he lacked ambition, far from it; he just seemed quite content to do assistant work whilst he finished off his doctorate. He worked extremely hard, had the perfect temperament for lab work and, ultimately, I enjoyed having him around.

"Was Rachel here when you came in this morning?"

"Who?"

"Rachel."

"Who's Rachel?"

I must still have been sleepy because I didn't register the bizarre nature of his question for a few seconds.

"Rachel...my partner..."

"Alex, I don't know who you're talking about, but nobody else was here when I arrived."

"Ok..." I replied, still thinking that my sleepiness must be rendering me only semi-intelligible this morning.

I looked around to see if you'd left me a note of some kind, but there was nothing. Anyway, if you had been here why did your side of the bed look like it hadn't been slept in? No, that much was clear: for whatever reason you hadn't come back here last night. I realised that I'd left my phone upstairs. Maybe there was a message there from you. As I headed back up to get it, Phil looked up again.

"I haven't gone out for coffee yet, figured I'd wait 'till you showed up. I'll go along to the shop in a minute, do you want your usual?"

"Yeah, sure..thanks Phil".

I headed back upstairs and found my phone on it's charging plate next to the bed. There were two messages from Ray, my supervisor over at the University, telling me to call him as soon as possible this morning and a missed call from him. There was also another missed call from a number that I didn't recognise, but nothing from you. Now panic began to set in. You hadn't come back here and you hadn't called. I wracked my brains to try and remember if you had had something special on the night before:

Dinner with colleagues from the department? - no, that was last week.

Was your brother in town? - I didn't remember you mentioning it. Drinks with your friends? - yes, that could be it...no, wait, what day was it? Friday. You normally went out with them on a Wednesday evening...unless you had decided to meet yesterday, instead. Anyway, you normally came back here afterwards...unless you decided to go back to your flat...though you didn't usually...

I was still cradling the phone in my hand as I went through all this in my head. I looked across at the bedside table and frowned. Something was different about it. I kept staring at the objects on there trying to work out what had changed. Then it hit me.

The picture.

The photo of you and I, that your brother had taken at your parents' place two Christmases ago, was no longer there. I walked over to the table again to see if it had fallen down the side somewhere but it hadn't. I looked around the room. Had I moved it somewhere else when I'd tidied up the bedroom last? I couldn't see it anywhere. Taking the phone with me, I went into the sitting room but I couldn't see it there either. I headed back into the bedroom and opened the clothes cupboard.

Looking back, I don't know why I did this. The chances of the picture having been put in the cupboard would have been pretty slim, to be honest, so I don't know why that seemed like the next most obvious place to look.

The picture wasn't the only thing that wasn't there anymore. All your clothes were gone too.

It wasn't as if you kept that many clothes at my place: a few pairs of underwear, 3 or 4 pairs of socks, two bras, two tops, one spare pair of jeans and an old pair of tracksuit bottoms that you liked to change into in the evening, after work. As your flat was so much closer to the campus where you worked, it never made much sense to keep more than a handful of clothes here; but now they had all gone.

I ran back into the bathroom. Only one toothbrush in the holder beside the sink, only my shampoo and shower gel by the side of the bath. I pulled the bathroom door closed and found your bathrobe was no longer hanging on the hook behind the door.

I sat down on the edge of the bath. My hands were trembling slightly. I dialled your number on the phone and put it to my ear. *Pick up, please pick up… whatever happened, we can fix this.* The phone rang and rang. No answer. *What had I done to make you leave? Why couldn't I remember anything about what had happened?*

I heard the front door close downstairs. Was that Phil leaving to get the coffee or coming back with it? Then I heard voices. I walked over to the stairs hoping that it was you, but it wasn't. The voices were both male. One was Phil's, the other belonged to Ray. They were talking very quietly, it was hard to make out everything they were saying:

"...she seems pretty groggy, that's all..."

"....understandable, given the circumstances..." Ray replied.

Then then I heard Ray say "Rachel". I couldn't hear what he said exactly, but the name rang out like a starting pistol to my ears.

"What about Rachel?" I asked, walking down the spiral staircase.

"Hello Alex, how are you feeling this morning?"

"I'm fine, Ray. What are you doing here?"

"Coming to see you, of course, just like we agreed yesterday."

"I don't remember scheduling a meeting with you today..." I began, but then I remembered the more pressing question on my mind: "What were you saying about Rachel?"

"Phil said you were asking about her"

"Phil didn't know who she was, Ray...what's going on, where's Rachel?"

"Calm down, Rachel's where she normally is..."

"What are you talking about Ray? She didn't come back here last night, all her clothes are gone, her picture...what the hell's going on?" I felt dizzy, the neck pain came back suddenly. I gripped the handrail of the staircase. Ray must have noticed this.

"Just take it easy, Alex...why don't we just sit down, eh?"

He helped me over to the old leather sofa in the corner of the lab. Once I was sitting down he turned to Phil.

"You said you were just about to go out for coffee, Phil. Why don't you do that now, I'll stay here with Alex."

"You're sure?" asked Phil. He looked genuinely concerned.

"I'll be fine," Ray replied. "Oh, and get me a cappuccino while you're there, huh?"

"Sure." Phil hesitated for a second and then picked up his jacket and headed out the door.

"Do you feel dizzy, Shall I get you some water?" Ray asked, looking at me like a doctor.

"I'm fine, there's a bottle of water over there by the side of the fridge that's mine..."

Ray got the bottle of water and came back again.

"You should drink some more..." he said, handing me the bottle "...it'll help with the dizziness."

"I told you, I'm not feeling dizzy anymore. What's going on Ray? Where's Rachel?"

"Don't get yourself worked up again..." he pulled up a lab stool and sat down opposite me. "How much can you remember from last night?"

I thought for a minute. "I was working here with Phil, until about 4pm, then I had a shower, then..." I paused.

What did I do after that?

"And after the shower?" Ray asked, that doctor's look in his eyes again.

"I...I don't know."

"Do you remember meeting me, for instance?"

"No...did I?"

"Yes."

"What were we meeting about?"

This was odd. Ray and I had worked together for many years now, but we rarely socialised, aside from the odd faculty function. He had a wife and two fairly young kids at home and lived fairly close to the campus. I was based downtown. We were colleagues, not friends.

"We'll come to that in a moment, Alex. First, I'd like to ask you a few basic questions, if you don't mind?"

"Why?"

"Humour me..."

"Sure," I replied, still not sure where he was going with this.

"What's your full name?"

"Oh, c'mon Ray..."

"What's your full name, Alex? This is important."

"Alexandra Jane Wells"

"Date of birth?"

"March 22nd 2010"

"How old are you?"

"28."

"What day is it today?"

"Friday May 14th."

"Do you have any brothers and sisters?"

"C'mon Ray, this is ridiculous..."

"Please just answer the question, Alex..."

"No, you know I don't - I'm an only child."

"What do you do for a living?"

"I'm a neuroscientist, specialising in the study of human memory, based out of the University."

"Be more specific, Alex. What's the nature of your research into memory?"

"A study of the hippocampus and the process by which memories are stored and recalled."

"Ok...What would you say if I told you, you'd just created a break through, equivalent to that of Kandel or Nader?"

"I think I'd remember that..."

Ray laughed. It was a sudden, loud, roar of laughter. The laughter of someone hearing something unexpectedly hilarious.

"Did I say something funny?"

"No, no..." he said, drying his eyes. "it's not funny. really... Ok, last question: Does the name 'Rebecca' mean anything to you?"

"No..." there had been a Becky Felton, who had sat next to me in Kindergarten, she was the last "Rebecca" that I could remember being on speaking terms with. "Should it?"

"I guess not."

"You said you'd tell me about Rachel."

"Right..." he paused, searching for the right words. "I don't know how to say this other than just to tell you straight out, ok? I'm afraid, you're going to have to prepare yourself for a shock..."

Oh, no. No, no, no...

"Rachel's dead, Alex."

"What! How?"

"It was a car crash. They think the other driver drifted across to the other lane and hit Rachel's car head on. She was killed instantly. They never found the other driver."

"No, no, that's not possible, she hardly ever drove...When did this happen?"

"3 years ago, Alex, don't you remember?"

"Wait a minute, that can't be..."

"It's the truth, Alex...think about it..."

I tried to focus on a detail, any detail, of Rachel in the last few days:

I brought a coffee up to her in bed, one morning.

I watched the sunrise from the windows of the lab while I was doing this. It was one day last week, wasn't it?. No, maybe the week before... within the last month,

> *(five years ago)*

> > *surely.*

"It's not true, she was here...just the other day..."

"No, she wasn't Alex. Think carefully."

"I am! She was here, I'm sure she was."

"Yes, Alex, she was. 3 years ago. Not since. Think about it. Think about it *carefully.* Try and remember..."

But, I wouldn't. I was already up on my feet, searching for something, *anything*, that would prove him wrong. There was an old CD player in the corner of the lab, almost nobody uses them anymore and Phillips officially ceased to manufacture any more players after 2028. We'd kept ours, partly because Rachel and I had so many CDs between us that we loved and couldn't be bothered to re-buy in another format. We kept it down here because I liked to listen to music whilst I worked in the lab. I went over to the cd rack, looking for something specific: Keith Jarrett - Paris Concert. I mostly listened to classical music whilst I was working in the lab, the Jarrett was an exception. Rachel had bought it for me as a birthday present last

(one)

year after finding it in a second hand shop and it had been played often since then. She'd written a message on the case:

'*To my darling Alex,*
Something different. I hope you like it,
Happy Birthday,
love,
Rachel'

She'd written the date underneath and that's why I wanted it now. I searched the CD rack for its distinctive crimson spine, cursing myself, silently, that I still hadn't gotten around to putting the discs in alphabetical order...

"What are you doing, Alex?"

"I'm looking for a CD, just give me a second..." I scanned through each CD spine in turn.

Where was it?, Was it there staring me in the face and I just couldn't see it?

"What does a CD have to do with any of this?..."

I heard the jingle of Phil's keys as he came back from the coffee run.

Phil, of course! He was generally the one who selected the music we listened to in the lab. Maybe he had put the CD somewhere else and that's why I couldn't find it... I turned around and saw him standing there next to Ray, the coffees in the little cardboard holder tray they give you when you have to carry more than two. I rush over to him, presumably looking like a crazy woman judging by the look of fear in his eyes. I take the tray of coffees out of his hand and give it to Ray and then pull him over to the CD rack.

"Phil, have you seen the Keith Jarrett CD?". Phil just stood there. I could see the beads of sweat beginning to glue strands of his long black hair to his forehead. His eyes were even larger than before, he glanced quickly at Ray.

"What CD?"...

"Keith Jarrett - Paris Concert. Dark red cover, Jarrett's name and the title on the front in big blue and white letters...it's a solo piano cd..."

"You t-told me to get rid of it," he stammered.

"What! that was one of my favourites...when?"

"About a month ago... I put it on and you got mad, don't you remember?"

"I got mad at you, for putting a CD on?" Suddenly I realised that I was gripping his arm tightly. I let him go. He looked terrified.

"You went apeshit, you ran over to the player, pulled the disc out and threw it across the room. Told me to throw the CD away."

For the second time that morning, I felt genuinely scared. I could tell by the look in Phil's eyes that he wasn't making this up, but I had no memory of this whatsoever. I looked over at Ray. He's got that doctor's look again: calm...detached, even.

He knows something about this.

"What's going on, Ray?"

"Everything's going to be ok, Alex. Have your coffee and I'll explain everything."

I walk over to him and take the proffered cardboard beaker containing my usual lactose free Latté with one sugar and sit back down on the sofa. I sip the coffee and recoil slightly at the taste.

"Arggh... Phil, I think they've given me soy milk again, instead of lactose free..." I take another sip to make sure, but my headache's coming back again. Now I start to feel woozy. I look up at Ray. He's watching me carefully.

"Everything ok, Alex?" I wanted to answer, but my eyelids were starting to feel heavy.

"Coffee..." is all I can manage to say. I try to get up from the sofa. It's not easy, my legs wobble precariously as I try. Ray gets up, alarmed.

"Take it easy, Alex, just sit down and finish your coffee, then we can talk..." He tries to get me to sit down again but I push him away, dropping my coffee cup as I do so. It hits the floor and splatters the bottom of Ray's trousers and his expensive-looking brown leather shoes.

I don't know exactly what made me do what I did next. Was it that sudden look of fear that I saw in Ray's eyes, that told me he'd put something in my coffee whilst I'd been talking to Phil? Or was it something more instinctive that told me I had to raise my knee as he bent down to retrieve my fallen cup? Whatever the reason, my knee made contact with Ray's forehead. I didn't even raise my knee that much - three inches at the most. Perhaps it was the combined force of my knee coming up to meet his forehead as he went down quickly, perhaps it was the fact that he crouched down, rather than bent down, that sent him reeling back against the refrigerator with such a crash, that all the contents rattled.

I didn't stop to find out.

Phil was just standing there across the room, mouth wide open with his coffee still in his hand as I leapt over Ray's out-stretched legs and hurtled towards the front door. Fortunately, Phil hadn't locked the door when he'd returned with the coffees, otherwise I'd have been sunk. My own keys were still safely tucked away in my jacket pocket in the hall cupboard and there would have been no way to get them before either Ray or Phil regained their composure and tried to wrestle me to the ground. As it was, neither of them had the time to do anything because I was out of the door and down the stairs into the bright sunshine of the street below in a matter of seconds.

2

Behind the old factory complex, where my home and lab were located, there's a small network of alleys leading between the various buildings. It was into these that I ran after leaving the building, hiding myself behind one of the metal refuse bins there. My sprint down to street level had used up the last of the adrenaline surge that escaping from Ray and Phil had brought on and now I found myself shaking and wheezing uncontrollably. I struggled to get my breathing under control as I knew the others couldn't be far behind.

Sure enough, I had just managed to quieten my breathing when I heard the sound of running footsteps coming down the alley in my direction. Ray and Phil stopped a little way past where I was hiding, but in the confined space of the alley I could hear everything they said.

"She's not down here," said Phil, who was almost as out of breath as I was.

"She can't have gone far. I gave her a strong sedative, she didn't drink much of the coffee, but it should at least slow her down a little. Plus, she has no travel pass, I.D. or wallet with her. How far can she get without those?"

How far indeed. I had nothing on me but the clothes I was wearing. *What was I going to do?*

"Let's head back to the street. You go left, I'll go right. Check every doorway or side alley you find. When you get to the end of the block, cross over to the other side of the street and double back. Alex must be somewhere nearby."

"And what if I find her? Supposing she gets violent again?" Phil asked, sounding worried.

"This is Alex we're talking about, remember. What happened back at the lab was my fault, I shouldn't have tried springing the truth on her like that. She got scared that's all. I never expected the side effects would be this severe. If I had, I would never have let her go home again last night. Keep your phone on, if you spot her, just call me and stay put. We'll tackle her together."

"You know, this would all be a lot easier if you just told me what the hell is going on..."

"I can't, Phil. Believe me, it's best you don't know more than you have to. Suffice to say Alex's latest experiment has succeeded on a level none of us could have ever dreamed of and now we really need to find her and get her sedated as soon as possible. Come on..."

The two of them turned and headed back the way they had come. I stayed there crouched behind the bin for another minute or so listening to their footsteps die away. Then I stuck my finger down my throat and forced myself to throw up whatever sedative was still inside me. I felt better afterwards, certainly less woozy. I leaned back against one of the bins and considered my options: It would probably take them at least 10 minutes to go up the street, checking every possible hiding place on the block. If they 'd left the door to the lab and my apartment unlocked that might just give me enough time to nip back in and grab my wallet, I.D. and travel pass before they came back again. It was risky as hell, but I didn't really see that there was any other option. Ray was right: I wasn't going to get very far without those 3 items.

Since the beginning of the 21st Century, a gradual increase in the world's paranoia fed by politicians and pandemics had resulted in a variety of restrictions on freedom of movement. I.D.'s for every citizen were now compulsory and, like many urban areas, the city had been divided into zones with checkpoints at each to track those moving between one zone and another on foot. Add to that, a universal Travel Pass uniquely linked to everyone's I.D. meant that travelling across zones using other methods of transportation was also regulated. With less people commuting, this could be carried out far easier than before. Being caught on the street without an I.D. meant you were immediately taken into custody for questioning. In short, without an I.D. and travel pass I was going nowhere.

I squeezed out from my hiding place and checked the alley. The coast seemed clear. I moved cautiously back towards the street. I could see no sign of either Ray or Phil once I got there, so I headed up the stairs to the lab. As I'd hoped, the front door was closed but not locked. I slipped inside, closing the door again behind me. I went straight to the hall cupboard, where my jacket was hanging. My wallet and keys were there in the pocket, just like I remembered. I checked inside the wallet to make sure my travel pass was there - it was. I couldn't find my I.D. though. I checked both the pockets of my jacket for the familiar plastic card attached to it's lanyard, but it was in neither of them. Had I left it upstairs, when I'd gotten undressed? It was something I often did when I was tired, forgetting about the little card hanging around my neck until I got into bed.

I raced up the spiral staircase to the bedroom. I had no idea how long it had been since Ray and Phil had gone off to check the street. At least 5 minutes already, perhaps even 10. The chances were high that they'd be returning any minute now and I'd be trapped. I found the I.D. hanging by its lanyard from the back of the chair where I'd hung my clothes the night before and stuffed it into my pocket. I grabbed a gym bag from the cupboard in the bedroom and threw a few pairs of socks, an extra bra and some underwear into it. Then I ran to the bathroom and packed a toiletry bag containing my asthma medicine, toothbrush, toothpaste, some tampons and a pack of ibuprofen from the small cabinet above the sink and headed back downstairs to the lab.

I took 2 bottles of water and a couple of chocolate bars from out of the fridge and caught sight of my phone still lying on the lab counter. I debated with myself for a few seconds whether or not to take it with me, before scooping it up and tossing it into my jacket pocket with my keys. I turned and walked towards the door and was about three steps away from it when I heard footsteps outside. In a panic, I turned and ran back to the hall cupboard. I had just managed to squeeze myself into a corner behind some coats when I heard the front door open and Ray and Phil's voices once more.

"So what do we do now?" I heard Phil ask.

"I'm not sure, just let me think for a moment...I still don't think she'll have gone far, but obviously with only two of us it's not that easy. I'll have to call Matheson, I guess..."

"Who is Matheson?"

"The guy from the government agency that's picking up the tab for this whole affair."

"So this is a government funded operation?"

Wait... What?

"Who do you think could have paid for all this, the University?"

"Well, I guessed some of the money must have come from elsewhere...but the government? With this sort of tech? I mean...the implications...Did Alex know about this?"

No. Alex most certainly did not.

"As I said before, Phil: it's better that you don't know all the details. Hey, where's Alex's phone?"

Oh no. I immediately found my phone in my pocket and switched it off completely.

"She had it in her hand earlier, when she came downstairs. I remember seeing it when you helped her over to the sofa."

"That's right, good. If she still has it in her pocket then perhaps we can track her..."

"How are we supposed to do that?"

"Through Matheson. I'll call him now. Do me a favour: collect together any hard copies of the research, all the portable drives from the computers and put any specimens from the fridge into cold storage boxes, we'll need to take anything of value with us when we go."

They were packing up the lab, leaving nothing to chance. I heard Ray open the front door and step out into the hallway to make the call. I inched forward and opened the door slightly. Phil was busy by one of the computers with his back to me. The entrance to the fire escape stairs was at the other end of the lab just behind the spiral staircase, but could I really reach it without Phil spotting me? The chances seemed pretty slim, but if I stayed where I was they were going to catch me sooner

26

or later and I certainly preferred my chances against Ray and Phil than I did against some government agency.

I opened the door a little wider, I had to check where Ray was. If he'd pulled the front door closed when he went out I had a chance. If he'd left it wide open and was standing right outside he'd spot me straight away. I crouched down on the floor and peered through the gap between the cupboard door and the floor. I could just make out that the front door was more or less half closed and beyond it, glimpsed Ray's shoes as he paced back and forth whilst on the phone. I looked back at Phil again. He still had his back to me. It was now or never.

Opening the door a little more and, keeping as low as I could, I crept forward across the hall to the lab counter in front of the refrigerator. From there, I crawled as quickly as I could on my hands and knees over to the small recess where the lab counter stuck out 15cm further than the wall next to it. I was now almost directly opposite the spiral staircase, with the window that opened out onto the fire escape less than a metre away to my left. Then I heard Phil walking back across the lab to the refrigerators just in front of me. I froze. There was no way I could make it across to the window now without being seen. Phil took a cold storage bag from one of the shelves above the sink and went to empty the fridge directly opposite me. He jumped and turned around when he saw me right behind him, reflected in the glass door of the fridge. He opened his mouth to speak but I put my finger to my lips and he stopped. I could see the fear in his eyes and I hoped he could see it in mine. I beckoned him over to where I was crouched. He hesitated for a second, then inched his way over, warily.

"What are you doing back here?" he asked in a low whisper, "are you crazy?"

"I needed my wallet and stuff, please don't turn me in."

"I don't know what you did Alex, but this is serious. Ray will be back any second. What's all this about the government being involved?"

"I knew nothing about that, I swear. Ray was the one dealing with the funding, he only told me that it came from outside the University. Please, Phil...I can't remember anything from last night, what happened?"

"We worked until 4, then you told me to finish up and go. It was like you were anxious for me to get out of here or something..."

"Did I say anything about what I was doing or where I was going?"

"No, I just assumed you were going out somewhere. I thought maybe you had a date, judging by the way you were anxious to go and have a shower and get changed..."

"Did I mention someone called 'Rebecca'?"

"I thought you said your partner's name was Rachel?"

"It is... did I mention a 'Rebecca', either yesterday or before?"

"Not that I remember, but then you never mentioned Rachel before today, either..."

"Never?"

"Not once."

A chill went down my spine. The odds of Phil not having met you at least once in the 2 years he'd been working for me, were extremely low. The odds that he could have gone all that time without hearing me mention your name, at least once, were next to zero.

"Look, I'm going to go. I'm sorry all this happened Phil, I will do everything I can to sort this out, I..." I wanted to tell him what a good assistant he'd been or how good it had been working alongside him for the past two years, but I didn't get the chance because at that moment Ray came back.

I pulled my knees in as far as I could and to his eternal credit Phil edged himself closer to the end of the counter to shield me as much as possible.

"Matheson just triangulated the signal on Alex's phone and says it must still be here somewhere. We have to find it before we leave."

I pulled the phone out of my pocket and placed it in Phil's right hand, hoping I wouldn't make Phil jump as I did so. He handled it like a pro.

"I found it while you were outside," he said, handing the phone to Ray. "It was on the floor by one of the computers...Alex must have dropped it during the scuffle."

"Great, that saves us some time." Ray sounds like he's dealing with nothing more serious than a faculty meeting running late. "How's the packing up coming along?"

"I've collected all the drives and I'm just packing up the specimens. Maybe you could just grab any hard copies lying around?"

"Sure," Ray replied.

"I think I saw a bunch of papers over by the CD rack, actually. I don't know if they're anything we need to keep." *Well done Phil. Send him over to the other side of the lab, maybe then I can get out of here.*

"I'll have a look..." I can hear Ray moving over towards the CDs. I start to move towards the window but Phil quickly pushes me in the other direction - towards the still open front door. I make it across the gap between the lab counter and the partition wall that separates the front door from the far end of the lab where the CD player is. I hear Ray's voice again: "Oh and Phil, make sure we have all the chipsets with us. We can't leave a single one of *those* babies behind..."

"There's one missing," Phil said. I froze.

"Really? Did you notice that just now?"

"No, I saw there were only five this morning, when I came in. I meant to ask Alex about it but with everything that happened...I forgot about it again until now."

I don't know what made me touch the back of my neck as soon as Phil said that. Intuition? The memory of this morning's headache? I lifted up my hair at the back and there it was just under the base of my skull: a small line of sutures. Recent surgery.

Someone had implanted one of my own chipsets into me.

"That's nothing to worry about..." Ray said, his voice like a doctor's once more. "I have the other chipset at my office on campus, I forgot - Alex gave it to me."

"It was here yesterday, when I left."

Don't push your luck Phil. You're dealing with a man who illegally implanted a chipset into one of his scientist's brains and lied about who was funding this whole operation.

I was by the door. I should have been gone already, but I wanted to hear what Ray had to say.

"She gave it to me yesterday evening. I wanted to show one of the prototypes at a meeting to fund the next stage of the project's development."

Wow, what a salesman this guy is! No wonder I fell for it.

"What exactly did you do to her yesterday, Ray?"

"I've already told you it's better you don't know all the details..."

I backed out of the front door as quietly as possible and then made my way quickly down the stairs and back out onto the street again.

3

I headed into the alleys again, cutting through the various old factory buildings in a zig-zag in order to reach the monorail station on Vernon Street. Strictly speaking the station on the corner of Parker and 3rd Avenue would have been nearer, but it had the disadvantage of having an electronic barrier between the street and the station where I would need to swipe my travel pass. At Vernon Street there was no barrier. There, you went up the stairs to the platform and weren't expected to swipe your pass until you were on the train itself. I planned to get on the train and not swipe my ticket, hoping that no ticket inspector came along in the meantime, get off 2 or 3 stops before my destination and walk the rest of the distance on foot. Any government agency that could track my phone would certainly be checking the activity on my travel pass and I didn't want to find them waiting for me when I arrived.

Another reason for heading through the back alleys was that I hoped it might hide me from the thousands of surveillance drones that continually hovered over the downtown area. With Matheson's involvement these would soon be tasked to look for me as well.

I reached the station, climbed the stairs and saw that the next train was due in 2 minutes time. There was no-one around as it was nearly 11 am and the few commuters there were would have long since reached their place of employment. I sat down on a bench, pulling the hood of my sweatshirt over my head in an attempt to shield my face just a little from the myriad security cameras installed in every station. I felt sure Matheson would be keeping tabs on all the public transport near my house. I had no idea what sort of sophisticated the facial recognition software they might be using so, fearing the worse, I kept my hood up and my head down.

I ate one of the chocolate bars from my bag and took two ibuprofen, chased down with half a bottle of water. I felt the sutures at the base of my skull again. None of this made any sense.

The train arrived and I got on, pretended to swipe my pass and sat down on one of the side-facing seats, hoping that my hood and the angle might stop my being immediately recognised on one of the security cameras. I leaned forward, with my elbows on my knees and closed my eyes.

Somebody had implanted a chipset into my brain.

The chipset was a microscopic motherboard, barely 1cm in length, that formed the cornerstone of my research into memory and its functions.

It built on the work of both Karim Nader and Christine Denny. Nader had discovered it was possible to rewrite the memory of a lab rat, trained to fear a tone that heralded a small electric shock, by using Anisomycin - a drug that blocks the proteins needed to create connections between synapses. This meant the rat was no longer able to recall the memory that caused it to fear the tone. Denny had used mice whose genome had been genetically modified to include DNA from light-sensitive Algae. Denny's work, which she christened 'Optogenetics', involved using a drug that told any brain cells that fired during the hour when the mice enjoyed a positive experience of playing in a friendly, safe environment, to install the light-sensitive DNA onto those cell's surfaces. After a while, the drug would wear off but the cells would remain light sensitive. This meant that Denny could later make the mice "recall" the pleasant memory, even in a situation where they would otherwise be frozen in fear, by using fibre optic lasers to shine light directly into the mice's brains causing the light sensitive parts to react. In other words, triggering positive memories with the flick of a switch.

Nanotechnology had progressed significantly in the years since Nader and Denny's pioneering work and so instead of genetic modification or fibre optics, I was able to design the chipset. Encased in a layer of organic tissue, it could be implanted easily into the hippocampus, the area at the bottom of the brain where memories are created. It transmitted wireless data about which synapses in the brain fired when a certain memory was recalled. That wasn't the clever part though: The chipset could also receive wireless data, so you could also use it, in combination with a drug such as Anisomycin, to 'import' memories into your brain, with the drug helping to wipe the parts you no longer needed.

This one piece of technology could hold the key to successfully treating Alzheimers, Dementia or damage to the hippocampus brought on by head trauma. I'd also invented a way of making anyone change their mind and believe whatever I wanted them to. That's why Phil had been so scared when Ray had mentioned government funding. The technology was only in its infancy but already the potential for its misuse was practically limitless: Silencing embarrassing witnesses, controlling politicians or the media (not that they needed much help there), creating unquestioning obedience in members of the armed forces, assassins that could be triggered like *The Manchurian Candidate*...the list went on and on.

At this point, knowing how dangerous the technology could be in the wrong hands, you could be forgiven for asking why on earth I would ever have wanted to build such a thing. The answer was simple: It was the latest destination on a journey that had begun when I was 7 years old.

Computer lessons had always been my favourite and I often got to class slightly early. That morning, I had walked into the computer lab at school and found our teacher, Mrs Bradbury, standing over one of the computers, frowning. She had looked up as I came in the door.

"Oh hello, Alexandra, come and sit down at one of the computers - just not this one, though please. It keeps crashing. I'll have to try de-fragging it, maybe that'll solve the problem."

It was a word I'd never heard before and I asked her what it meant.

"Well, you see a computer's memory is a bit like ours - it doesn't store everything in one place. It breaks up the information and stores in various different parts of the hard drive. It does this when there's not enough space to store the information as a complete unit. After a while, if there's too much information in there that's fragmented, the computer starts to run slower or maybe even crash because it's searching for these little bits of files. Defragmenting it puts the separate pieces back together as much as possible."

We've all heard the cliché: *it was like a lightbulb went on in my brain.* Well, cliché or not, that's exactly what happened here. My brain lit up like one of Denny's genetically modified mice. I had never even considered how my brain or anyone else's might function. Without knowing it, dear old Mrs Bradbury had shown me not only me a glimpse of my future, but also stumbled upon an important area of contention within the scientific community involved in the study of human memory.

Serious scientific study of how our memory works is still relatively young, though certainly a little older than Mrs Bradbury herself (I can't say how old she actually was back then - to a 7 year old, anyone over the age of twelve seems ancient).

Brenda Milner began her pioneering work with her patient, Henry Molaison (known as H.M.) in 1957. Molaison had had parts of his hippocampus surgically removed in order to elevate the constant seizures he'd suffered since a childhood accident. However, whilst it did relieve the seizures, the operation resulted in the disturbing side effect of Molaison being unable to create new memories. This seemed to confirm that the hippocampus was the area of the brain responsible for memory creation.

The question of how this actually happened was taken up by Austrian-born neuroscientist, Eric Kandel. Using large sea slugs he was able to actually show, on a single cell level, a stimulated sensory neuron creating new synaptic pathways with a motor neuron. In other words: the physiological change that takes place within the brain when new memories are formed.

The point that Mrs Bradbury inadvertently raised was what happens to those connections that are created. The prevailing theory from the time when Kandel published his findings was that, once created, these synaptic connections remained fixed. This was called 'consolidation'. 'Consolidation' suggested your brain was much like a huge public library and every memory had its specific location within the shelves. You might forget where the location was or forget that this particular 'memory book' was even included in the library at all, but it was still there in its original place, just waiting for your mental librarian to rediscover it.

Karim Nader's work changed all that. If his rats could be made to rewrite their memory of fearing a tone, then it meant that the act of recalling a memory also made synaptic connections. In effect, every time you recall a memory you change the connections in your brain - the books in the library were constantly changing their location on the shelves, every time they were borrowed. This new theory, which was hotly debated, was called 're-consolidation'.

Re-consolidation shed new light on the work of Elizabeth F. Loftus, a cognitive psychologist who'd begun studying the unreliability of the human memory as far back as the 1970s and who coined the term "the mis-information effect" to describe the way a person's memory of a specific event could be influenced by post-event information. All memories are susceptible to change due suggestibility or a conflict with another person's recollection of the same event.

Loftus' work was demonstrated brilliantly in a study that Julia Shaw and Simon Porter published in 2015, where they were able to get 70% of the participants to falsely remember committing a crime in their past. They used a combination of real details amongst the lies that they told the participants, re-enforced with cognitive exercises where they would be asked to visualise aspects of the story. The results spoke for themselves: If you could already implant a false memory through suggestion and visualisation, how much more vivid would those memories be if you could somehow beam those false scenarios, directly into the brain itself? That's where the chipset came in.

This was clearly what had been done to me. It was the only logical explanation. How else could I have forgotten that you died 3 years ago? There was an easy way to check: I could go to your flat, near the campus. If someone else now lived there, I'd know the truth. Although, that still wouldn't answer the bigger question: Why?

We'd already tested versions of the chipset in mice and rabbits with complete success, but we were still a long way off getting permission for human trials. *What purpose would implanting it in me possibly serve?* Surely, if Ray and or Matheson had wanted to push forward with human trials it would have been easy enough to find a volunteer from within the military and then just fake a break in and steal a chipset.

Why did they need it in me?

I got off the train at Rainbow Park, 2 stops before yours at Ellis Avenue. I walked down the steps to the Butler Street exit, bypassing yet another barrier which would have necessitated swiping my Travel Pass. I crossed over the street and cut through the park, which seemed to be full of children on a school field trip. Across the street from the park's north entrance was the house where we first met at a party.

I'd gone because I couldn't think of a decent excuse not to go. Michelle, the woman who'd invited me, was a Psychologist at the University. I wasn't that keen on her personally, but she'd invited both Ray and I when we'd bumped into her at a faculty meeting the week before and neither of us had felt able to refuse.

There were a few people there that I vaguely knew from the University, but I'd spent most of the evening hiding in the kitchen because Michelle seemed quite intent on pairing me off with her older brother - a pleasant enough man who seemed just as mortified by his sister's matchmaking as I was. I had just been musing about the fact that I often seemed to end up in the kitchen at these sort of parties, when you came in. You got yourself a glass and picked up the open bottle of red that was on the table.

"Any good?" you asked, looking over at me who already had a glass of it in my hand.

I shrugged. "It's a bit light for a Primitivo, if you ask me, but at least it's drinkable and it's the only thing they had, other than beer."

You poured yourself a glass, held it up to the light and then put the glass to your nose.

"Wow!" I said, "a connoisseur..."

You smiled and I can still remember the warm tingle that smile gave me. You tasted the wine and looked at me with an expression that said: 'Yeah, I can drink this...'. Then you walked over to where I was standing. I held out my hand.

"I'm Alexandra, but everyone calls me 'Alex'."

"Rachel...Who are you hiding from, Alex?"

"What makes you think I'm hiding?"

"You're drinking a bottle of wine by yourself in the kitchen. That's generally what I do when I'm trying to avoid someone."

"Ok, I'll admit it - I'm hiding. Michelle seems to be trying to set me up with her brother."

"Oh dear... she's always trying to pair him off with someone, poor guy. Last time it was with me."

"What did you do?"

"Oh, he was more embarrassed than I was and apologised for his sister - apparently their mother put her up to it."

"Sounds like their mother and mine would get along..." There's that laugh and the warm tingle again. "Do you work up at the University too?"

"Yes, I teach Literature and Creative Writing...you?"

"Well, I'm based there, but I mostly work out of my own lab, downtown."

"Wow, you must be well funded..."

"Well, sort of... I already had the space: two floors of an old factory building, I live on the top floor and wanted to use the lower one as a workspace. The

42

University helped me fit it out with the stuff I needed. It made life a bit easier for them too because lab space is already scarce on campus."

"I'm sure lab equipment isn't that cheap. I take it you're on a grant?"

"Yes, even the University's pockets aren't that deep."

"I've got a friend of mine who's bought an apartment in a reconditioned factory complex downtown, the prices on those places are skyrocketing. How on earth did you manage to afford two floors?"

"I got in early at the start, 3 years ago. Everyone thought I was crazy."

"I'm guessing they don't think so anymore?"

"Well, my mother constantly worries what I'll do if I ever have children, but I guess she doesn't count."

"No..." you replied, laughing, "all mothers are like that. Mine too, but then I only live in a small apartment near the campus." Another smile. One more and I think my heart might burst.

"You know, if you're interested, I'd be happy to show you my lab sometime..."

"The lab that's also your apartment?"

"Sorry...that didn't come out quite the way I meant it to..."

"No, no don't apologise. As *Do you want come back to my place?'* lines go, that's pretty smooth..."

I must have blushed despite laughing, because you noticed it straight away.

"Wow, a physiological reaction!"

"I beg your pardon?"

"You're turning red, I've embarrassed you..." You paused. I dared to look up from my shoes and into your eyes once more. "What's your field?"

"I'm a neuroscientist, doing research into human memory."

"Remembrance of things past is not necessarily the remembrance of things as they were."

"That's true."

"It's Proust."

"Who?"

"Marcel Proust..."

"Oh, right!...He wrote a series of books about memory or nostalgia or something, didn't he?"

"You're studying memory and you've never read Proust?"

"I'm slightly ashamed to say that I haven't..."

"Only 'slightly'?"

"Ok, then 'very ashamed'..."

"You don't need to go that far, most people haven't read him."

"You have."

"Yes and I can also say that, having read him, I have no desire to do so again."

"You're not doing a very good job of selling him to me."

"That's because I'm a Lit professor and not a bookseller." More laughter. "But, I can lend you a copy of one of his books if you're really interested..."

"Ok...Maybe we can meet up for a coffee next time I'm on campus?"

"Sure... or you could just come to my apartment."

"*Your* apartment?"

"Yeah, I know, it's not as smooth as saying: "*why don't you come and visit my lab*", but I guess it'll have to do." My turn to smile this time. You lean in close and kiss me. Not a long kiss, it lasts barely a second. An initial experiment to test your findings. "Do you want to get out of here?"

"Sure..." I replied and we did.

That's where it started.

4

4 blocks from the North side of the park was Mount Pleasant Street, where your apartment was. Approaching it this way, I came at the street from the opposite direction than I would have, if I'd gotten off the Monorail at Ellis Avenue. Halfway down the street I could see that I'd made the right decision. Across the street from your apartment block sat a large S.U.V and a Transit Van. The S.U.V had darkened windows and no license plate. Not a good sign.

I ducked into a doorway and watched for a while to see if anyone went in or out of your your apartment or one of the vehicles, but no-one did. I turned and walked back down the street the way I had come. How could I have been so stupid? Of course they'd be waiting for me at your place - that was the most obvious place for me to go. I turned left at the top of Mount Pleasant Street and headed Northeast for about 5 or 6 blocks, keeping to the side streets as much as possible. There seemed little point in asking about you on campus, as they were sure to have staked that out as well. The only other place I had left to check was your parents' house. I just hoped that Matheson (or whoever it was) wouldn't be waiting for me there as well.

I'd been to your parents' house a few times, generally at Christmas. I could never remember the house number, but always recognised the front door, which had been painted dark blue. They lived in the once highly fashionable suburb of Boyeton, where you and your brother had grown up. Now, with the return of a large percentage of the population to the downtown areas of the city, lots of families had sold up and moved. I thought of my own parents in a similar situation in my home town. Had Ray or Matheson already contacted them? What story had they been told? Had my mother been shocked to hear that her daughter (the one she boasted to her friends was doing important work that could benefit the whole of humanity, even though she herself couldn't make head nor tail of it) was being sought by the government? Did she protest and say: *No, there must be some mistake, my daughter's a scientist. She couldn't possibly be mixed up in any sort of trouble with the government. If that were the case she would know...*

But she wouldn't, because I didn't even know, myself.

I managed to get on the monorail again at Williams Street without swiping my pass, going in through the exit on the south side of the station. Once again, the platform was practically deserted and I could only hope that I wouldn't run into a ticket inspector on the train itself. I would have no such luck at Boyeton, however, as it was at the end of this particular line. I could get off the train a stop or two before like last time, though the stops were much further apart out in the suburbs and that would mean at least a 30 minute walk through some unfamiliar neighbourhoods where I would stick out like a sore thumb. I decided to chance it and wait until Boyeton. No inspector appeared, so I waited until the stop before - Linden Road - to swipe my pass. Not swiping it at all would have meant the barrier wouldn't let me through at Boyeton. I just had to hope that Matheson wouldn't be able to mobilise his agents fast enough to get to Boyeton before I got clear of the station there.

That was assuming he didn't have people waiting for me there, already.

The platform at Boyeton looked reassuringly empty when the train pulled in. I walked out slowly through the entrance hall to the barrier, swiped my pass and went out on to the street.

Your parents' house was about a 10 minute walk from the station. To be on the safe side I took a less direct route, cutting through Wellsley Park.

Some years ago, when we'd visited your parents, you'd taken me for a walk around your old neighbourhood, including the park, whose west side was directly opposite their house. As a child, as soon as you'd been old enough to cross the road safely, the park had become an extension of your home and you and your brother would play there every day after school until it got dark. I'd marvelled at the level of freedom you'd been allowed. Even out in the relatively tranquil neighbourhoods like Boyeton, the days of letting your kids play outside unsupervised until dark were long gone. My own mother would have never countenanced such a thing and had frequently gotten worried if she'd been unable to spot me playing in our own garden from the windows of the house.

You had no idea about the park's history, but you told that its name had come from the now disused well, that still stood in front of a small wood that covered most of the park's Northeastern corner. You'd guessed that it was a hangover from Boyeton's earliest days as a small village. The wellhead was now cemented over but you'd told me that, when you were a child, it had only been covered by steel grating and children were warned never to climb on it, in case it gave way and they ended up plummeting 70m down the narrow shaft. You also told me about how your brother and some of his friends had gottten a reward when they found a woman's purse and handbag, which had obviously been stolen, amongst the bushes just behind the well. The woods had seemed like a forest to you and your brother then. At various times it had been Endor, Mirkwood and Sherwood Forest and as Maid Marian you had your first ever kiss. The boy, a friend of your brother's, had been so surprised that he'd run off home in tears. We'd both had a good laugh about that.

No kids played in the park now. The school that both you and your brother had gone to at the south entrance to the park had long been relocated. The park itself had become overgrown and a little neglected in the intervening years. I tried to imagine it in its heyday with a little 10 year old version of you, climbing trees and hiding behind bushes with a toy bow and arrow in your hand, but I couldn't.

I cut through onto a path where tennis courts had once resounded to volleys of shots between opponents. Now they stood silent with a field of weeds growing through the cracks in the asphalt. The bushes on either side of the path that led out of the park had grown so much that the gap between them had almost disappeared.

I didn't remember the park being quite so unkempt, but it had been at least a year

(4 years, actually)

since I'd last been here. I pressed myself up against them on one side and cautiously checked out the street on the other side. Your parents' house was almost directly opposite. It looked deserted. The whole street did. I moved slowly forward towards the line of birch trees that separated the park from the street itself. There were no cars on the street at all. I looked across at your parents' house again. From this new vantage point I could see that the dark blue front door had been boarded up, just like the others. The street had been abandoned.

This should have clinched it. Your parents had long since moved away. The house that (*seemingly*) so recently had been full of life and the festivities of a family at Christmas was now just an empty shell. Something made me want to investigate it further, however. I crossed the street, went up the little side alley next to the house, opened the gate and went into your parents' back garden.

The garden, once your father's pride and joy, was now horrendously overgrown. The lawn, which had clearly had not been mown in more than a year, almost came up to my waist. The greenhouse, where he'd once shown me the various species of tomatoes he was growing, had become a makeshift aviary for several groups of birds. A nearby crab apple tree had obviously blown over in a storm, and demolished part of the roof in the process.

The back door to the house had been boarded up as well, but I managed to pry the boards loose and break the window enough with a stone to reach in and unlock it from the inside. I closed the door behind me and walked through the dusty, deserted kitchen to the hallway and the stairs.

Your room was at the end of the landing. You'd told me that, as a teenager, you'd meticulously worked out where you had to tread to avoid the creaking floorboards, as you made your way past both your parents and your brother's rooms when you came home late from a club. I suspected that would be less possible now, as every step I took resounded through the empty house.

The door to your room was ajar, I opened it fully and peered inside. Aside from the dust and the peeling wallpaper, it looked the same as I remembered it. Your bed, which the two of us had found uncomfortably small when we'd visited for Christmas, still sat in the corner by the window. I moved over to the window and looked out across the street to the park. *Was that someone moving over there in the shadows by the trees?* I strained my eyes to try and see but it was almost impossible to make anything out with the sun streaming in.

I remembered lying in this bed watching the sun rise through your bedroom window. It must have been that same Christmas. You'd gotten up early and snuck downstairs to bring us coffee in bed. For a brief moment, lying there in the bed next to you, I'd had this wonderful sense of what it must have been like to grow up here. I could just imagine the teenage you lying on this bed, engrossed in a book. This house was part of what made you the confident person you were. There was no sense of having to live up to someone else's expectations, like there was in my house. Your parents and brother were lovely and had made me feel as if I was part of your family. Lying there, bathed in the winter sunshine, I'd felt completely safe and loved.

"It was stupid of you to come here, Dr Wells..." I spun round and saw a figure sitting in the rocking chair next to the open door. "Ray thought you'd be cleverer than that, but I knew you'd turn up here eventually." He leaned forward a little from the darkened corner. He was a man in his early 50s or thereabouts, dressed in a suit that looked expensive.

"Matheson?" I asked.

"That's right."

"How did you get in? The front and back doors were..."

"Boarded up?...We're a government agency, doctor. If we weren't able to break into people's houses without leaving a trace then we wouldn't be very good at our job, would we?"

"I guess not. You must have been waiting here a while."

"An hour or so, but we knew you were on your way."

"How? I didn't even know I was coming here an hour ago. Wait a minute...the chipset...you tracked it's wireless signal didn't you?"

"For a scientist, you're not particularly bright, are you?...Wireless signals are limited by transmission power, antenna type, even the environment... Yours is limited even further by it being encased inside your skull, making it practically useless as a tracking method unless you happen to be within about 40 feet of me. No, I knew you'd come here because there's only a few places you would logically go...Ray thought this might be a long shot but that's why I thought you were even more likely to come.

"If you knew I'd run then why didn't you put a team in place to catch me leaving the lab?"

"I did, they must have arrived shortly after you'd left…I must say, it's a great shame you chose to involve Phil. He asks too many questions and now he knows about the missing chipset, it's only a matter of time before he puts the pieces together."

"What are you going to do to him?"

"That depends on Phil and how well he is able to listen to reason."

"And if he won't?"

"He will be silenced, one way or another."

"What about me? Will I even get an option or will you just kill me, here and now?"

"I'd much sooner not have to kill you, Dr Wells. It would best for everyone if you just came along quietly now, so we can quickly and painlessly remove the chipset and analyse the data. You'll be handsomely compensated for your outstanding contribution to science, who knows maybe you'll even win the next Nobel Prize?" He paused, seizing me up. "The alternative is: I shoot you, remove the chipset during an autopsy and your work will simply disappear, just like your corpse. It's your choice."

"I could rush you, try and wrestle the gun from your hand. You're less than 3m away, can you get the gun out of your pocket quick enough to shoot me in that time?"

"Stop being ridiculous, Dr Wells, you're a scientist, not Lara Croft."

"Maybe I feel I've got nothing to lose..."

"Then you've been watching too many movies. People like you always have something to lose, that's why you're going to come with me now. However, if you're still feeling mutinous, let me give you a little incentive..."

A jolting pain went through my neck. My whole body convulsed and I collapsed to my knees.

"Impressive isn't it?..." Matheson said, rising from the chair and holding a small silver box in his hand. "I had some of my tech people make this up for me. It causes a couple of the components within the wireless receiver in the chipset to short each other out momentarily, creating a very mild electric shock to your brain. Like having a mild seizure." He pressed the button on the small box again. Shapes swam in front of my eyes and my neck felt as if someone had clamped it in a vice. "Still want to try and escape?" he asked, as my vision began to blur and I passed out.

5

I woke up strapped to a chair in a room surrounded by bright lights. I was wearing a hospital gown. A woman in a lab coat was examining me. She looked familiar, though I couldn't think why. My throat was dry. I licked my cracked lips and tried to swallow, even though it hurt to do so.

"Are you Rebecca?" I croaked.

"No," she said, smiling. "I'm Doctor Burgess, the neurosurgeon you asked to implant that chipset in your brain..."

"*I* asked you to implant it?"

"That's right," she said. "I'm also the one who's going to try and remove it in a couple of hours, once I'm satisfied that you're fully recovered from whatever Mr Matheson did to you." She shone a small torch into my eyes and got me to follow her finger, as she moved it back and forth. "Do you still feel dizzy or nauseous?"

"Thirsty..."

"That at least is remediable. Here, drink some water," she said, holding a beaker with a straw in front of my mouth. The water trickled down my throat and after a few seconds the pain in my throat subsided a little.

"How's she doing doctor?" Ray had come in and was looking at me with his arms folded.

"She seems to be fine, now..." Burgess replied. "I'll leave you two to talk. Just let me know if she starts to feel nauseous again and don't get her worked up."

"I'll do my best, doctor," he said, as she left the room. "Well, Alex you certainly gave us all quite a scare..."

"Is that what I did? Did your precious little experiment get out of control?"

"Our experiment, Alex, even though I know you don't believe me..."

"Would *you* believe you, if you were me?"

"Probably not. That's why I want to show you something."

"What?"

"The truth, Alex. From someone you will be able to believe." He wheeled over a flatscreen monitor on a small trolley and pressed play on the small media drive next to it. The video file opened and suddenly I was watching myself talking to the camera.

"My name is Dr Alexandra Wells," the me on the screen said. "I'm making this video as a record of what I'm about to attempt. The date is Tuesday May 13th. In a few minutes, I will go into an operating room and under general anaesthetic will have a chipset that I have developed, implanted into my brain by a neurosurgeon. Once there, the chipset, which is embedded in the hippocampus, will enable me and my team to rewrite specific memories within my brain. We've made several tests on both mice and rabbits and I have volunteered to be the first ever human trial of this technology. The memory that we will try to rewrite is the death of my partner, Rachel Ballard, who died 3 years ago in a car accident. The treatment involves several stages. Firstly, I will try to recall in as much detail as possible, the events surrounding Rachel's death. The chipset will record the specific synapses that fire during this period of recall. Then, using a combination of cognitive exercises and imagery, we will use the chipset to rewrite these particular memories with the aid of Anisomycin to block the proteins involved in recalling the old ones. The final stage is sleep. This allows the brain to rest and during this time the new neural pathways will become fixed. I want to stress, once again, that my participation in this experiment is voluntary and I have not been coerced into doing this in any way. I am of 'sound mind' and have signed a legal waiver absolving the other participants of any responsibility should something go wrong, either during the operation or as a result of the memory rewriting process."

The video clip then switched to footage of the operation. I watched as my anaesthetised body lay face down on the operating table, with my head supported as it might be in a masseuse's chair. I felt a phantom tingle up my spine as I saw them make a small incision in the back of my skull, the grey white of cranial bone clearly visible under the crimson folds of cut back skin. Then, going in under the occipital bone and through the large opening at the base of the cranium, I watched Dr Burgess attached the chipset to my hippocampus. Ray fast forwarded through the rest of the operation and the video now switched to the memory rewriting procedure. I was strapped to a chair, much the same as I was now, a drip hooked up to my arm and Ray seated in front of me. He went through a series of cognitive exercises, designed to recall my memories of Rachel's death: Where I was when I heard the news, what I was wearing, what the policemen looked like who came to tell me about the accident. This was interspersed with visual images of newspaper and tv reports about the crash projected onto a screen in front of me. Throughout this, he would stop periodically to check the results on a computer monitor next to him. Then the second stage of the procedure began. The Anisomycin was administered and Ray began a second set of cognitive exercises, this time designed to replace those memories of Rachel dying.

I looked across at Ray, who was studying my reactions as I watched all this. Only then did I feel the tears streaming down my face. He paused the video.

"What's wrong, Alex?"

"None of this tells me why..." I mumble, as I felt the tears trickle down on to my neck.

Ray got a tissue and dried my eyes like a parent comforting an upset child.

"Rachel's death haunted you. You never told me why, but for some reason you blamed yourself for the accident. You kept working, but it kept pulling you down. You tried every type of therapy you could think of, eventually resorting to the bottle. Your behaviour was becoming erratic. The outburst over the CD was just one in a growing chain of incidents where you'd completely lose it. Something had to be done. In a way, I was relieved when you suggested 'Rebecca'."

"Rebecca?"

"'Rebecca' was our code name for this project, after the old Hitchcock film - the man haunted by the memory of his dead wife."

I nodded. Rachel had loved both the film and the book by Daphne Du Maurier that it was based on. She regularly included as part of the reading list on her course on the gothic novel. In the story though, Rebecca is a manipulative woman who tricks her husband into killing her so that she won't die slowly from cancer and somehow the knowledge of this made me uneasy.

"Feeling a little better are we, Dr Wells?" Matheson had just walked in, looking a combination of smug and impatient. "Realised that we're all on the same team now?"

Go fuck yourself, you supercilious prick. "It seems so..." I replied.

"Good. Better for everyone that way."

"Better for you, certainly."

Now, now, Alexandra, don't be so hostile... After all, once Dr Burgess has removed the chipset, you can go back to your normal life and your work will be celebrated throughout the scientific community."

"They won't be celebrating me once they discover I gave the technology to the government."

"They won't know, that's the beauty of this whole exercise. In a few moments, you and Ray will go through the whole memory re-programming procedure again. All knowledge of Project Rebecca will be removed from your memory and you will wake up in your own bed again tomorrow morning with a slight hangover and the memory of a great party celebrating the success of your work; which Ray, of course, will verify. Next month, your research will be published in several journals and your reputation as one of the great scientific minds in your field will be assured."

"While you quietly get a head start on developing the tech for military or law enforcement purposes..."

"Exactly."

"What about the missing chipset, the one that's in me? Won't I notice it's gone?"

"We've already had a duplicate made." said Matheson, smiling.

"And you're ok with this?" I ask turning my attention back to Ray.

"It's a necessary evil, Alex. Plus, the way I see it, as soon as we publish our findings the government would be on to us about using the tech for the same purpose. This way at least, we've been able to benefit from the association."

"You'll forgive me if I'm having trouble seeing what those benefits are."

"Don't be so naive. The funding that we've received because of this project is substantial. It's keeping the entire faculty afloat in a time when every other University is struggling to get grants. This is far bigger than just you and I. When your work is published we will be at the vanguard of scientific research in this country."

"What about Phil?" I asked Matheson

"He has sensibly agreed to co-operate."

"I doubt you gave him a lot of choice..."

"He has the same amount of choice you all do," Matheson replied. "This project and its work will continue with or without any of you. Keeping your mouth shut in order to reap the benefits shouldn't be much of a decision."

"He's right, Alex," Ray chimed in. "We've come this far, let's see it through, ok?" I nodded, reluctantly. There didn't seem to be any other option left to me.

"Good," said Matheson. He turned to Ray. "Start the re-programming procedure."

Matheson left me alone with Ray, once more. We went through the same thing as before. Ray used cognitive techniques and video surveillance of me, presumably provided by Matheson, to cover everything I'd done in the last day. Then a nurse inserted an IV drip into my arm and we began going through my fake memories of the party: what I was wearing, who was there, what I had to drink and so on. I was having trouble concentrating, though. My head was beginning to ache again. Ray stopped and looked at me.

"Alex, are you ok? You look pale."

"I don't know," I replied. "My head's killing me, was it like this last time?"

"Maybe, but I don't remember you mentioning a headache." He gets up and hands me the beaker of water. "Here, drink some more… see if that helps." He puts the beaker to my lips, I take a sip and a blinding flash of pain hits me behind my eyes with such force, that I wince and the water dribbles out of my mouth again.

"Alex! Are you ok, what's wrong?" I can hear Ray's voice but it's muffled and far away. Words swim in front of my closed eyes and I read the text.

Dr Wells is a liability. Suggest terminating her whilst we have the chance. Will make all the arrangements with Dr Burgess. We can make it look as if she died on the operating table - Matheson.

I turn to Ray, he looks pale too.

"Don't let them kill me, Ray…"

"Who? Alex, what are you talking about?"

I opened my mouth to speak but no words came out. I'm passing out and can't help but smile as I disappear into the lovely blackness of unconsciousness.

6

I woke up without you again.

This time I hadn't expected you to be there, though.

The light was dim and what I was lying on wasn't very comfortable.

It was also damp.

I was in a forest. I sat up. Everything felt stiff, but my head felt much better. I was wearing some kind of uniform. I looked down at my hands. They were covered in dried blood.

What had I done?

I heard a small rustle in the bushes on my left and saw that a deer was watching me. We looked at each other for some time. Eventually, satisfied that I presented no immediate danger, it put its head down to graze again.

I looked at the uniform. There was an identity badge clipped to the belt of the trousers. I unfastened it to look at it properly. It was a man's uniform that apparently belonged to a security guard called Donald Heinlein. He worked at somewhere called Whitehaven Labs. I'd never heard of the place, though I guessed it was where Matheson had taken me. I studied the photo of Mr Heinlein hoping for some fragment as to how I'd come by his clothes and badge, but nothing came. I looked at the blood on my hands.

Was this his or someone else's?

I stood up slowly, bending my legs in an effort to get rid of the feeling of pins and needles in both of them. The deer ran off, quickly. I looked around. I was in a small clearing, created where the surrounding trees had either fallen or been cut down at some point in the past. The overhanging branches of those that remained were dense enough so that very relatively little light shone down on to the mossy forest floor.

Having no idea which way to go, I decided to head in roughly the same direction as the deer. The pins and needles had now subsided and given way to a dull ache. I went slowly, as there was a lot of bracken that constantly got caught around my feet. Several times I heard the familiar whine of a surveillance drone and ducked behind a tree or crouched beneath a bush, in the hope that I wouldn't be spotted. Each time the drone seemed to pass overhead without stopping, so I figured it hadn't seen me. Eventually, the ground began to get steeper and I found myself having to scrabble on all fours up the side of a grassy bank. I'd hoped that the higher ground might provide me with a better vantage point to be able to see where I was, but the trees were so thick that it was impossible to see much further than about 50 metres ahead. I sat down against a small birch tree and rested.

I felt like I'd walked for several hours but it was probably only one. My throat was dry and my head ached again because I hadn't had anything to drink. I'd need to find either a way out or some water soon or I'd start to feel faint from dehydration.

I heard movement and the sound of twigs snapping behind me. I moved back behind the tree a bit more and waited. I saw nothing at first and wondered if it had just been another deer. Then two men wearing camouflage gear came out from the trees below. They had automatic rifles. They paused at the bottom of the grass bank and one of them spoke into his walkie talkie.

"This is C group, we're in grid sector 17, we think we may have picked up her trail. Over."

The walkie talkie crackled in response. "Roger that, C group. Use caution. Over."

The camouflaged man spoke again. "Roger, Control. Over and out." He turned to his partner. "What do you reckon, should we try going up to the top this ridge and see if we can spot her?"

"That's going to be hard in this sort of dense woodland. Show me the map again..."

The first man pulled a handheld device out from his jacket. He showed it to his partner. "We're here, this is the bank. It seems like it continues at that elevation for about a half click in each direction."

I leaned over the edge of the bank a little more trying to get a glimpse of what they were looking at. His partner examined the device as well.

"Seems like the trees are pretty thick up there, could be a good place for her to hide..." he said.

Then the strangest thing happened. My head ached and I felt the same wave of nausea like I had in the lab with Ray. Suddenly, I could see the whole terrain of the forest stretched out in front of my eyes, like a topographic wire frame model overlaid across the landscape. In my mind, I could adjust the scale and angle. I could see how the land rose and fell. I could see in every direction at once even though I couldn't see further than 50 metres in any direction, with my actual eyes. I knew that to my left the thick trees only continued for maybe another 200 - 250 metres before they opened out onto a clearing where there was little to no cover. To my right they stayed thick for much longer, continuing even as the ground began to slope down towards a small stream. This was the way I needed to go in order to stay hidden as long as possible and the stream would provide me with water. I became aware of small triangles slowly moving across the terrain in pairs. It took me a moment to realise what I was seeing, but then it became clear: They were search teams like the one just below me. I looked again at the direction I wished to go in. There were no triangles in the vicinity of the stream. If this whole process had taken more than a few seconds I might have stopped to wonder how any of this was possible. As it was, I had no time.

"Hey what's wrong with this thing?" The second camouflaged man was smacking the side of the handheld device with his hand. "Seems to be picking up some kind of interference..."

The walkie talkie crackled again. "C group, do you read? We've just picked up neural transmissions interfering with your wireless device, the subject is within 30 feet of your current position..." The two men immediately looked up and caught a glimpse of me as I ducked back out of sight.

"Roger that, Control," said the first man, "we've spotted her, engaging now. Over..."

"Roger, C group. Repeat. Use caution. Over.".

The second man was already scrambling up the bank. Like me, he was forced to go down onto to his hands and knees as he neared the top. I needed to act fast. I spotted a large stone at my feet, picked it up and threw it as hard as I could at the first man, who was still at the bottom of the grass bank. It hit him squarely in the middle of the forehead as he was beginning to raise his rifle. A single shot rang out as fell backwards, firing into the air. The second man was almost at the top of the bank now, but the noise made him turn and look. I seized this chance and aimed a kick at his head. It connected with his jaw and sent him tumbling back down the bank, joining his partner in a crumpled heap at the bottom.

I got up and ran headlong into the trees to my right. The topographic view of the forest appeared in my head once more and I could see pairs of little triangles coming towards me from all sides. However, the route to the stream was still clear and I pushed on towards it, trying not get caught up in the low hanging branches of the trees. After about 10 minutes I found the ground beginning to slope down gently on the right and followed it down for another 5 or 10 minutes before I began to hear the tell-tale sound of running water. A few more seconds and I glimpsed the stream through the trees and ran to it. Lying flat on one of the rocks at its edge, I cupped my hands and scooped as much water as I could into my mouth and onto my face. The shock of the cold water made the headache and nausea subside a little. After a few minutes of constant drinking, I rolled over on my back and lay on in the sun on the wet stone.

The map swam in to view again behind my closed eyes. One pair of triangles seemed to be following from the direction in which I'd come, but they were hindered by the thickness of the trees. Another pair was approaching from the opposite side of the stream, a little further down on my left. They were much nearer. I estimated they would reach the tree line in the minute or so. I needed to move. The safest option seemed to be to cross over to the other side of the stream and follow its course, upwards, to my left. The stream, though quite deep, was barely 4 feet wide and I was able to jump across it quite easily. I made my way quickly into the trees on the other side and was well hidden by the time I could hear the voices of the other search team crossing over the stream. Despite the fact that they probably wouldn't be able to hear much of anything over the running water, I kept low and tried to make as little noise as possible. The ground began to slope upwards again. I crested the hill but continued to follow the path of the stream as it cut through the forest. The sun was now directly above me, so I guessed it must be close to midday.

As I walked, I had time to ponder the bizarre nature of what had just happened. The chipset had been able to hack into the wireless transmitter of the handheld device the men had been carrying. Presumably, this had also been what had happened back at the lab when that message from Matheson had appeared in my head. Once there it seemed as though I could recall it at will, with the information updating itself live. It was as if my brain had been force paired with the device.

How was any of this possible?

My head began to ache once more and the nausea was slowly returning. I closed my eyes and looked at the mental topography that swam into view once more. I was heading upstream. All the triangles were, for the moment, a safe distance away and seemed to be converging in the opposite direction from where I was going. I decided to risk heading back down to the stream, to get some more water.

I kept thinking about what could have happened to allow the chipset to do this. Had something gone wrong, causing it to function in this way? Was this a side effect of something Matheson had done to me when he short circuited it? Perhaps, although, surely his tech people would have been smart enough to spot that possibility? The feelings of pain and nausea that seemed to accompany it worried me far more than the effect itself. Would they increase? The first time had felt far worse than now, perhaps the shock of it had been the reason I'd passed out. Yet I'd still managed to function. I'd obviously escaped and there'd been some sort of struggle - enough for me to end up with dried blood on my hands. I checked the map in my head again, compressing its scale this time. At the far side of the forest, more or less in the direction from which I'd come, there were large buildings. Some sort of facility. Whitehaven Labs, no doubt.

Was it because I was concentrating on the lab's location, on finding the route I'd taken to escape, that brought it all those memories back with such a rush? I couldn't tell you, but the pain that came screaming into my head at that precise moment was immense. It caused to me to fall to my knees and roll the rest of the way down the slope to the stream. The slow undulating wave of nausea that had been building became a tsunami. I retched uncontrollably, for several seconds. Regular migraine sufferers will tell you that the headache and nausea is often accompanied by severe visual distortions:

Shapes in front of your eyes smear and run like watercolour paints. This was like that but a hundred times worse and overlaid on top of these distortions, the map of the surrounding terrain and lots of little triangles changing direction, heading back towards the stream.

I pulled myself along on my belly towards the bubbling water a few feet away. If I could reach it in time, I hoped the shock of the cold water might revive me enough to help me keep going. I hung one arm over the stones on the bank and scooped a handful of water and brought it to my lips, then wiped my face with my cold, wet hand. It felt good but my eyelids were already beginning to droop. My head suddenly felt like a great weight pulling me down. I was slipping into unconsciousness again. The triangles were getting closer, but the pull of the blackness was stronger. Ray's worried face came back to me as I slipped away.

"Don't let them kill me, Ray..." I muttered again, as my vision darkened and I slipped back into the past.

Z

"Who, Alex? What are you talking about? "Alex?...Alex, can you hear me?" Despite how little I remembered afterwards, I had only blacked out momentarily. Ray leant over me and as he did, my arm came up, grabbed his jacket and pulled him close to me.

"Untie me..."

"Alex, you're not making any sense," Ray said, trying to free himself from my grip. "Let me call Dr Burgess..."

I tightened my hold on him, pulling him in closer.

"Untie me, Ray, we only have a few seconds before they get here."

Whether it was the look in my eyes or his own sense that something wasn't right, I don't know, but he reached down and undid the restraints that were holding me to the chair. I removed the IV drip from my arm. I could hear voices getting nearer outside the door. Dr Burgess and her team would be here any moment. Concentrating hard, I closed my eyes and suddenly it was looking at a schematic of the building. I knew the thickness of every wall, the location of each security camera, the electronic code to all the doors...

That was it.

I changed the door code. I could hear the struggle outside the door as Dr Burgess and her team found the access code no longer worked. My visual focus (if you could call it that) had somehow managed to split itself between my point of view from inside the room and what was happening outside the door, like watching multiple tv screens at once... except it really wasn't like that at all. There was no sense of separation between the events and images, like there would be watching more than one screen. The best way I can describe it is to ask you to imagine watching several films, projected at the same time but onto a three dimensional space instead of a flat screen.

In my mind I could see Dr Burgess calling Matheson on her phone to tell him about the door and soon he and his men would arrive to open the door by force. As she was doing this, I could see Matheson in his office reach into his desk drawer and remove the Glock 9mm automatic he kept there. He also picked up the little silver box from his desk and put that in his pocket. Once he'd finished talking to Dr Burgess, he got up from his desk and pressed a large button on the wall, triggering an alarm throughout the building. As he did this, I saw security guards all over the building, stop what they were doing and check in on their walkie talkies. Shutters slid over every exit and window. The building was being locked down.

Ray, realising the commotion that was taking place outside the door, had gone to try and open it himself only to find that was equally impossible. He was now shouting through the door to Burgess on the other side, trying desperately to make her understand that this wasn't his doing.

"Alex, help me open this door!" he shouted at me.

"Yes Alex, please open the door! We only want to help you..." came Dr Burgess' muted accompaniment from outside.

"I know what you want," I replied, "but I'm afraid I can't help you."

"Come on, Alex, this is ridiculous. We can't stay locked in here forever and there's no other way out of this room except through that door."

"That's where you're wrong, Ray," I said, standing up. My legs felt a little shaky under me but I could still walk. I went over to the far wall. There, about 15cm from the ceiling, was a ventilation shaft. A quick scan of the building's schematics told me it went back about 3m before connecting with another shaft running as far as the elevators, which had yet to be locked down.

I dragged a chair over to directly underneath the shaft. Standing on the chair I could just reach the vent. Now I just needed something to unscrew the grill in front of it. I searched through the drawers next to where I'd been sitting. I found a small pair of forceps and tried using the back end of the handle to loosen the flat head screws keeping the grill in place.

"Alex it's no use," Ray pleaded from behind me, "come down from there and let's be reasonable about this." I had already got one of the screws loose and was working on the second. If I could loosen that and one more, I would probably be able to slide the grill off the vent without loosening the last screw at all. Time was of the essence. The noise outside the door was growing. I could hear Matheson there now, his shouting muffled by the thick door.

"Dr Wells, this is your last chance: open this door or we'll break it down!"

Second screw loose, now for the third.

"I'm going to count to 5...1."

This screw was harder to loosen than the others.

"2..."

Ah, now it was coming.

"3..."

Out!

I swung the grill out of the way using the last screw as a hinge

"4..."

and pulled myself up into the vent.

"Alex, wait!" Ray said, but it was too late - I was already in the shaft.

"5...Right, we're coming in!"

I heard a terrific bang behind me as Matheson and his men attempted to shoot the lock off the door, but I didn't stop. It seemed to take them several tries and by the time they eventually got in I was almost by the elevators.

I peered into the elevator shaft. One elevator seemed to be further down by the ground floor, the other a few floors above me. I stopped and thought for a moment about the best course of action to take. The ground floor exits were securely locked down. I could have tried the parking garage and gotten out through there or at least hidden in somebody's car, hoping be driven out later. This seemed to leave too much to chance, however and there was a much higher probability that I'd be discovered before I could escape that way. I scanned the building schematics again, looking for a fire escape or an emergency exit that might perhaps have not been sealed off yet. Two floors up from mine was an emergency exit leaning to an outside fire escape. It was risky, but it certainly had better odds of success than any other.

I stretched out my hand to the lift cables. I would have to pull myself up using them and then try and swing myself into the ventilation shaft two floors above the one I was currently in. I just had to hope that nobody needed an elevator in the meantime. I clasped hold of the the cables, pulled myself out of the ventilation shaft using my arms and swung my legs on to the cable. Then I proceeded to try and pull myself up the cable using my hands and feet - not the easiest thing to do when you're only wearing a hospital gown.

Fortunately, there were support struts on the side of the shaft every one and half metres that I could put my feet on and rest for a few seconds before continuing. It took me a while but I eventually made it up to just above the shaft opening and tried to swing myself over to it. The first two tries I didn't get close enough. The third time I almost managed to grab it and on the fourth try I was able to cling on with one arm. There was a support strut within reach that I could just put my left foot on. With a final slight swing on the cable I was able to get near enough to hold on with both arms. I'd almost managed to pull myself up into the shaft using my arms, when I heard a loud clanking noise below me - one of the elevators was starting to move! With a last frenzied effort, I pulled myself up into the shaft and got my legs tucked in behind me just as the elevator roof drew level with the shaft.

As I lay there, panting for breath, I could hear the voices inside the elevator, quite clearly.

"She's bound to be somewhere on this floor." That was unmistakably Matheson's voice. "Fan out, check every room carefully - but remember we want Dr Wells alive, so taser her, don't shoot her!"

I heard a few mumbled sounds of agreement, the sound of the elevator doors opening and several people getting out. I moved slowly along the shaft, trying to make as little noise as possible. The second vent opening that I crawled past looked out onto a locker room. I tried pushing at the grill that covered the shaft opening.

It wouldn't budge at first, but then I leaned back against the shaft and tried pushing with my feet and it gave - a little. I pushed a bit more, conscious of not wanting to make too much noise and eventually the bottom two sets of screws came away from the wall. I changed position and wiggled the remaining screws free with my hands.

I was about to remove the grill, when I heard a noise outside the door of the locker room. I quickly stuffed the two screws back into their respective holes and slid back, out of sight of the vent opening. The door to the locker room opened and a security guard came in, taser in hand. He looked around the room and opened several of the lockers, despite the fact that nobody could have really fitted inside one. He seemed satisfied and turned to leave. He was almost at the door when the screws holding the grill in place gave way and the whole thing clattered to the floor with a loud clang.

The guard, presumably already on edge, freaked and turned and fired his taser without thinking. The wires shot out sparking in the air for a few seconds before falling to the ground.

"Shit!" he said and threw the taser on to the ground before unholstering his pistol. "Come on out of there, I've got orders not to shoot you but I can't promise anything if you try to rush me." He edged closer to the vent opening. I was far enough back that he couldn't see me at first but as he moved nearer, he could see my feet. "I can see you in there! Come on out slowly!"

My mind was racing, I needed to think of something fast. I closed my eyes and scanned through the building schematics in my head again - there had to be something I could use.

"If you don't come out then I'm going shoot through the wall into the vent. I'm going to count to five: 1..."

"Ok, I'm coming out, don't shoot!" I eased myself forward towards the vent opening. "I need to turn round and climb out backwards..."

"Ok, nice and slow," he replied.

I turned and climbed out of the shaft, legs first, with half of my brain concentrating desperately on a way out of the situation and the other half on how much of my naked body the guard was getting a glimpse of through the grubby hospital gown. My feet were almost on the floor now. I let go of the shaft and dropped to the ground.

"Put your hands on your head, slowly... don't try and turn round! Any sudden moves and I will shoot you!"

I still had my back to him. *Think, think! there must be something you can use... Wait, the fire alarms - that's it!* He moved closer to grab one of my hands and pull it behind my back. I could feel his breath on my neck. *Set off all the fire alarms in the building, do it now!*

The silence was broken by an ear-splitting roar of sirens and bells as every fire alarm in the building went off at the same time. The shock of this cacophony distracted his attention for a few seconds. That was all I needed. I brought the elbow of my right arm back sharply, smashing it into his nose and breaking it. As I turned around into him, my leftt hand caught hold of his right, which he held his gun in, stretching his arm out and upwards so he couldn't fire at me.

I had no idea how I knew how to do this. I moved smoothly, as if by instinct.

I was able to twist the gun from his grasp. Then we over balanced and went crashing backwards into the lockers behind. I managed to untangle myself from his grasp and struggle to my feet. I turned to face him and saw that he had smashed his skull on the corner of the lockers and a small but significant amount of blood was beginning to ooze from the back of his head onto the carpet. His eyes widened briefly, staring at me as he died. I just looked back at him, saying nothing.

With the alarms still ringing, I stood over his body and removed his clothes. He was slightly taller and bulkier than I was, so they were a little loose, but otherwise fit me well. His shoes were at least two sizes too big, however. I draped my hospital gown, which was now dirty from climbing through the shafts and up the elevator cable, over his semi naked body and tucked my hair in underneath his cap.

The alarms suddenly stopped. The guard's radio crackled into life: "All units report in.. Repeat. All units report in..." Several names called in from other radios.

"This is Heinlein, checking in". I said, in the deepest most masculine voice I could muster, whilst checking his name badge. I read his name again to myself:

Donald Heinlein. *'Don' to his friends, perhaps...*

This was the man whose life I had inadvertently ended. Did he have a wife and children? There was no wedding ring on the third finger of his now lifeless hand, not that this meant anything. He was young enough to presumably still have parents who would mourn him, perhaps even siblings. Tears came to my eyes.

What had I done?

I could have reasoned with 'Don'. Pleaded with him to let me go, perhaps even tried to escape down the vent shaft. If I'd thought of the fire alarms quicker, maybe that would have been enough to distract him whilst I escaped. He certainly didn't need to die. I closed my eyes and thought of the fire escape again.

Turn left out the door and then turn right at the end of the corridor. Third door on the left.

I needed to go before other guards arrived to check the rooms on this part of the floor.

"I'm sorry, Don..." I mumbled, as I turned away and opened the door to check that the coast was clear.

The corridor was empty. I moved towards the exit. I reached the door. I guessed it would be alarmed. I scanned through the building schematics again, found the specific alarm for the door and disabled it. I pushed the bar to open the door.

"That's far enough, Dr Wells..." said Matheson's voice from behind me. "We can't let you leave, I'm afraid."

I turned and looked at him. He had the Glock in one hand, his little silver box of tricks in the other.

"That uniform doesn't suit you at all. What did you do with Heinlein, is he dead?"

"Yes..." I replied. "It was an accident…"

"You don't need to apologise to me. Clearly, I underestimated your potential."

"That's what my potential is to you? Murder? Death and destruction?"

"Oppenheimer created death and destruction too, along with a formidable energy resource. Who knows what unexpected fruit your work will now bear. Work with us, Doctor. Help us understand what's happening to you."

"So I can end up dying on an operating table? I read your text to your superiors - no thanks."

"Don't be foolish, Alexandra. You're not Lara Croft, remember?"

I could see him toying with the silver box in his hand. I closed my eyes and looked into its circuits. I shorted several components and created new connections sending the current back into the case itself. When Matheson touched the button it sent the entire stored charge of the unit's lithium-ion battery into his arm, burning his hand. He let go of it with a scream and the box fell to the floor, smoking. I lunged towards him, smashed his other arm against the wall, making him drop the gun.

"Your little toys won't work on me anymore, you pathetic little man," I said, as I grabbed him by the throat and began to choke him.

"Alex, stop!" It was Ray. I could hear him running down the corridor behind me. "Please don't do this. Let us help you..."

"They don't want to help me, Ray, they want me dead. They were going to kill me on the operating table."

"You don't know that, Alex..."

"I do, Ray..." I grabbed Matheson's phone from the pocket of his jacket and tossed it to him. "See for yourself, the pin code is 4215. He sent a text message to his superiors. He had it all arranged with Dr Burgess."

Ray opened the message folder and read through Matheson's texts.

"Ok, I believe you. Now, let him go."

"What?"

"You heard me, Alex, let him go. His guards will be here any moment. You need to leave, now."

I released my grip on Matheson's throat and he sunk to the ground, gasping.

"You need to find someone you can trust to take a look at that chipset in your head and find out what's happened to it," Ray said, as he pushed open the fire escape door.

"I know..."

I heard the shot ring out. It made me flinch, but I thought Matheson's shot had gone wild. Then I saw the blood spreading across Ray's shirt. The bullet had hit him in the stomach. In my rage, I turned and kicked Matheson in the head. He slumped sideways, dropping the gun. I turned back to Ray, who was sliding down the wall, his fingers trying in vain to stem the bleeding. I went over to him and tried to put pressure on the wound, but he pushed my hands away.

It was his blood that had dried on my hands.

"Go! The gunshot will bring all the guards here any second now."

I got up and stumbled down the fire escape, 2 or 3 steps at a time. I was about 6 floors up. I was almost at ground level when I heard voices and footsteps on the metal steps behind me. I could see the perimeter fence and what looked like a forest behind it in the darkness. The shouts and footsteps were getting louder. I jumped the last few steps and ran. I turned a corner and headed towards the main gate. The guard on duty barely had time had time to shout in surprise as I ducked under the barrier and kept on running until I reached the edge of the forest.

Away from the bright lights of the compound and the perimeter fence, it was hard to see where I was going. I ducked behind a tree and tried to let my eyes adjust to the darkness. My feet were already aching from running in Donald Heinlein's oversized shoes. I could hear voices and footsteps behind me again and crept along further until I found a small bush and hid underneath it. The voices seemed to be all around me. Walkie-talkies crackled and several times I saw pairs of shoes pass by where I was hidden.

I stayed there crouching for some time, wondering when it might be safe to move. Eventually, I heard footsteps coming back in my direction and the voice of someone talking into their radio.

"Negative, there's no sign of her - we're heading back. We'll regroup and head out again at first light."

The footsteps passed on by and I waited for a good 10 minutes before coming out of my hiding place and heading deeper into the forest. I have no idea how long I walked or in what direction. Eventually I became aware that my head was throbbing and I sat down, meaning only to rest for a few minutes. The mossy ground felt cool under my head and after a few seconds I let the blackness of sleep replace the darkness of the forest.

8

My eyes opened again with a jolt. I had no idea how long I'd blacked out for - not more than a few minutes at the most, perhaps only seconds. I was still by the stream, the triangles were still moving towards me. My headache had lessened but it was not gone. I splashed some more water on my face and looked around me. I could see movement on the other side of the stream - one of the search teams would see me any second now. I closed my eyes and studied the terrain again, quickly. Other teams were closing in below me from the right.

I looked down at the bubbling water beneath me. It wasn't much more than a metre deep, but it was fast moving. I looked up and saw the search team reach the rocks bordering the stream on the other side. They were shouting into their walkie-talkies that they'd spotted me within in seconds.

There was no other way out. I rolled myself over and tumbled into the water. I was carried downstream quickly, bobbing under the water in some places. I could hear fragments of the surprised shouts of the search team as the water surged all around me. They were radioing frantically to other teams in the hope that one of them might be able to catch me as I came by. It was no use. None of them could get into position quick enough.

I continued my way downstream for what must have been several kilometres, before the stream opened up into a wider reservoir and the current slowed. I swam over towards one of the banks and pulled myself out of the water.

I lay on my back and closed my eyes. The topographic map swam into view once more. I was now 3 km northwest of the lab. The reservoir was at the very tip of one end of the forest. I got up and moved slowly through the trees on the bank until I came to some buildings on the far side. It was a garage and service station. Beyond that I could see train tracks heading in both directions. There was train depot that looked more or less derelict, presumably a throwback to when logging companies had used the area to transport timber in years gone by. I watched the garage for a few minutes. There was no sign of anyone either inside or out. I moved closer to peer in at one of the windows. I couldn't see anyone working. A "closed" sign hung on the front door and I just had to hope no-one lived in the rooms above. I picked up a nearby stone, broke a window and got inside.

There was a small bathroom behind the office in the garage. I used that to change out of my wet clothes and put on a set of overalls I found hanging on a peg. There was a fridge that didn't have much in it besides beer. I found a bar of chocolate in one of the cupboards and ate it hungrily. There was a map on the wall of the forest and surrounding area, which I studied whilst planning my next move. Looking at the map it was clear that the forest was located at least 40km away from where they'd captured me at Rachel's parents house, more or less north east from where I lived downtown. I was miles from anything. I looked at the train tracks on the map. Heading east, they skirted the forrest for about 5 or 6 km before heading into a tunnel and continuing on until Culverton. Heading west looked more promising. Following the stream as it continued its path after the reservoir, the tracks passed through an industrial district after 2km, before turning left towards Stanton. I might be able to find some sort of transport back downtown from there.

The bigger problem was where to go once I got back downtown. Ray had told me that I should get the chipset examined by someone I trusted and he was right. However, the number of people that could look at it with any sort of knowledge was small and Matheson would no doubt be watching most of them. My best option was Joanne, my former assistant. Whilst she'd left shortly before the first prototypes of the chipset had been completed, she'd been there for most of its development and would at least know what she was looking at.

I was distracted from my thoughts by a low hum, getting steadily louder and more resonant. After a few seconds it revealed itself as a helicopter, passing overhead. Was this more of Matheson's men? I looked out one of the windows to see if I could spot what direction it was going in. I was so busy looking, in fact, that I didn't hear the sound of a trigger being cocked.

"Those helicopters have been flying overhead half the night and most of the morning..." said a voice behind me. I froze. "My guess is they're looking for someone. Would that be you, by any chance?" I tried to turn around, but the voice stopped me short. "Stay where you are and put your hands in the air. Now, you can turn around, nice and slow..."

I did as I was told and found myself facing a tough-looking woman in her mid-50s pointing a shotgun at me.

"Please," I said, "I'm not looking for any trouble."

"Then what exactly were you looking for and why are you wearing an old pair of my husband's overalls?".

"I'm sorry... I just needed a change of clothes - mine were wet from the stream - and something to eat. I wouldn't have broken in if I'd known there was somebody here..."

"Well, of course you wouldn't," she said, raising the shotgun slightly. "No burglar wants people at home when they break in, do they?"

"Please... I'm really not a burglar. I don't mean any harm. If you'd just let me be on my way, I'll..."

"You stay right where you are!" she said, stepping forward with the gun. "You're not going anywhere until you tell me what you're doing here."

"My name is Dr Alexandra Wells, I was being held captive at a research facility on the other side of the forest. I managed to escape and now they're looking for me..."

"Who's 'they'?"

"Some sort of government agency... I don't know exactly. Please... they can't find me, if they do they'll probably kill me and anyone trying to help me."

She eyed me cautiously, wondering how much of my story to believe. She opened her mouth to say something, but before she could there was a knock at the front door of the service station. She looked at me and motioned to me to hide myself in the washroom. She leant the shotgun against the wall and went to see who was at the front door. I couldn't see who the person from my position behind the washroom door, but I could hear their voices clearly enough.

"Something I can help you with?" she said to whoever was at the door.

"We're searching for a fugitive who was spotted in this vicinity. I was wondering if you'd seen anyone hanging around here?" said the voice.

"Nobody hangs around here anymore, young man, this whole area's been forgotten since the logging trade dried up about 10 years ago. You with the police?"

"No, I'm from the government..."

"Didn't think so," the woman interrupted.

"Here's photo of the fugitive..." The voice continued. "She's a woman in her late 20s. Perhaps you'd take a quick look and tell us..."

"What branch?"

"I beg your pardon?"

"I asked what branch of the government you're from. Why should I tell you anything when all I have is your word that you are who you say you are? You haven't shown me any identification."

"I'm afraid I'm not at liberty to disclose which branch of the government I represent. As I was saying, the fugitive who escaped yesterday…"

"There aren't any prisons around here..." she interrupted again. "The nearest one's the other side of the county and that's for men only. I've got a no-good nephew who did time there a while back, so I should know."

"I didn't say the woman had escaped from prison, I just said she escaped." said the voice, cooly. "She's a mental patient who was undergoing treatment at a special facility near here. Now, if you wouldn't mind just taking a quick look at this photo, I'll be on my way."

"You can show me all the photos you like, sonny, I told you: I haven't seen anybody."

"Here's the photo..." said the voice, persisting. "Now, you're quite sure you haven't seen anyone who looks like this around here?"

"I just said that, didn't I?"

"You hadn't seen the photo then..."

"Because I didn't need to. Nobody comes up here nowadays, except the odd hunter looking to bag a deer."

"I see...would you mind telling me how long that window's been broken?"

The window. Oh, no...

"Oh, that! Been like that for months..." said the woman, without missing a beat. "I keep meaning to get it fixed - had a piece of board over it, must have fallen down again." Despite her quick answer, I thought I heard the slight tremor of uncertainty in her voice. I only hoped the man asking the questions did not.

"You should fix it, somebody might try to break in," the voice replied.

"Yeah, I know, but there's not much here that's worth stealing."

"Better safe than sorry..." said the voice. "Ok, thanks again for your help. Here's a card with a number on it to call if you should happen to see anyone who might fit this woman's description."

"Is there a reward or something if I do spot her?"

"No."

"Figures..." said the woman. "This government's too cheap to offer one. Folks are a lot more helpful when you offer a reward, you know..."

"I'm sure." said the voice, sounding bored now.

Good. Find her boring, you smug idiot, she's running rings around you.

"Thanks again for your help."

"No problem." the woman replied and I breathed a sigh of relief when I heard her close the front door. She walked back to the washroom and poked her head around the door.

"You can come out now, he's gone."

"Thank you," I said, coming out from behind the door, "you probably just saved my life."

"Well, don't thank me too quickly - he looked awfully suspicious, that one. Especially about the broken window..."

"I know, I'm sorry. If you give me your address here I'll send you some money when I get where I'm going, to cover the cost of the window and the overalls."

"Don't worry about it, the window won't cost much to fix and like I said those overalls belonged to my husband, before he died - I've got no use for them, now. Why don't you come upstairs with me and I'll see if I can find you some clothes of mine that might fit you?"

"That's very kind of you." I said "I'm sorry to hear about your husband..."

"It was his own stupid fault - the idiot!...had too much to drink and had an accident. Still miss him, though..."

"A similar thing happened to my partner, a few years ago."

"I'm sorry to hear that, honey." There was genuine tenderness in her voice now and I felt an immense surge of gratitude for this woman, who'd lied to protect me.

"Look," I said, checking the windows for any sign of movement outside, "I'm going to get going, thanks for all your help but I don't want to put you in any more danger..."

"I'm not in more danger than I am any other time - I can take care of myself - if anyone's in danger, it's you and you're about to walk right out into it again. Do you even know where you're going to go? There's not much around here, you know. If they catch sight of you from that helicopter you've got nowhere to hide."

"It's ok, I'm going to follow the stream until I get to this industrial district, here..." I said pointing at the map. "Then I'll either try and find a lift downtown from there or try and find somewhere to hide out for the night and start making my way towards the city in the morning."

"You'll never make it there. That guy that was just here, he won't have gone far. They'll probably have set up a road block stopping any cars going by, in case you hitched a lift with someone. Besides, even if you do make it, that industrial district's all but deserted these days - perfect place to corner you, shoot you and stick your body in some anonymous hole in the ground, where it'll never be discovered. Unless you're planning to go out like Bonnie and Clyde, you want to get to somewhere where there's lots of people."

"You seem to know a lot about this sort of thing."

"This isn't my first rodeo" she replied, with a slight twinkle in her eye. "As I said to the guy asking questions about you: I had a nephew of mine who was in prison for a while - until he broke out - I know a fair bit about manhunts and searching for escaped prisoners..."

"Ok then, what do you suggest I do?"

"First of all, you do nothing for the next couple of hours. Right now, they're looking for you throughout this whole area with everything they've got. If they don't find you within a couple of hours, however, they'll start redeploying their men elsewhere - that's when we'll make our move."

"We?"

"Of course! You're not going to get far on foot around here - best to wait awhile and then I'll drive you into the city, myself, once the heat's died down."

"I couldn't ask you to do that. It's too dangerous. What if we get caught? Then you'd be in danger too - This isn't the police who are after me. If these people catch us, they'll probably kill us."

"Then we'd better make sure they don't catch us then, hadn't we?" There was that twinkle in her eye again. "So, as we're waiting around for a bit why don't you come upstairs to the flat and tell me what we're up against, while I fix you something to eat. You look like you could use a good meal."

There seemed to be no arguing with her, so I agreed and followed her upstairs to the flat that she lived in, above the service station. It was small and clearly hadn't been redecorated in a while, but it was the most comfortable place I'd been in the past 24 hours. I gladly accepted her hospitality and took the chance to relax a little. She made me an omelette and I told her everything that had happened to me in the last day or so. In the process, she also told me some more about herself.

Her name was Judy and the service station and garage had been her and her husband's business until he died five years ago. Since then she'd kept it going by herself, more out of stubbornness than any sense of loyalty to her late husband. She'd never been much good at anything except fixing cars, she told me. She was always skipping school to help out at her father's garage, which is where she'd met her husband. He'd loved cars and engines just as much as she did. Everyone had said that there couldn't be a more perfectly matched couple. Walter, her husband, hadn't wanted to work for her father forever and eventually they'd bought this place. They had almost 20 years of doing the thing they both loved most in the world, until that one night when Walter lost control of his truck coming home from a poker night and ploughed headlong into a tree. With much of the population relocating back to the city from the suburbs, the business had dwindled to the point where she hardly bothered to open the garage anymore.

"But what else am I going to do?" she told me. Her parents were both dead, her only alternative would be to move in with one of her siblings. If she sold the garage, the money she'd get wouldn't even buy her a one bedroom flat, downtown. At least here, the mortgage was paid off and it provided a roof over her head. Between her husband's life insurance and the little bit of money she sometimes made restoring an old wreck, she got by.

"So tell me, Alex," she said after listening to my whole story and giving me the rest of an apple pie she'd made for dessert, "even if you get to your friend and she can find someway to help you. What are you going to do then? I don't pretend to understand much about this technology you've managed to develop, but it seems to me that this thing you have in your head is potentially so powerful you're going to be looking over your shoulder for the rest of your life."

"I don't know, exactly," I admitted. "Perhaps with Jo's help, we could leak it to the newspapers...though, honestly, I hadn't even got that far. The last 24 hours have just been about getting from moment to moment."

"Well, maybe you should start thinking about it and I want you to promise me something..."

"Name it." How could I refuse after the kindness she had shown me.

"Promise me you won't let them get hold of it."

"I'll try..." was all I could think to say.

"*Trying's* not good enough when the stakes are this high, Alex," she said, looking me in the eye. "You promise me you'll do whatever needs to be done to stop this falling into the government's hands, if it comes to it."

Killing myself, that what she was taking about. I could see her point, of course. Matheson had said himself that he didn't need me alive to acquire what he wanted from the chipset. After what happened at the lab, his men would have been given orders to shoot me on sight. Killing myself with a bullet through the back of my head would destroy the chipset and make sure that Matheson couldn't harvest it from my corpse.

"They still have the others that I made, as far as I know, they may even have made some more themselves."

"Then those will need to be destroyed too, if possible...but, from what you've told me, your one seems to be special. If the government gets hold of that, there's no telling what they'll do with it."

"I know. I wish I'd never invented the chipset now - I should have known someone would want to abuse the technology."

"What's done is done - you made it with good intentions - but now you know the truth, the only question should be: How do I put this right?" She looked at the clock on the wall. "It's been an hour and a half since that guy left. Why don't you lie down on the couch and try and get some rest for a while? I'll wake you in an hour or so and we can see about driving you into the city."

I did as she suggested and despite the couch being slightly too small for me, I fell asleep almost as soon as I lay down on it.

I can remember dreaming about you, of us lying in bed together. Then the dream changed. You were angry at me about something. I heard you talking quietly on the phone when you thought I wasn't listening.

Was this just a dream or was this a memory fragment coming back to me through my subconscious?

9

I was awoken by Judy shaking me softly.

"Wake up, Alex," she said, "it's time for us to go." She was kneeling by the side of the couch. "I let you sleep at bit longer as you looked so peaceful lying there, but we should go now before it gets dark. Go and have a quick wash in the bathroom over there. I've laid out some old clothes of mine that should fit you. We can't have you wearing those tatty old overalls, now, can we?"

I sat up and walked, bleary-eyed, over to the apartment's small bathroom. I splashed some cold water on my face and got changed into the clothes Judy had laid out for me. She looked me up and down when I came out.

"Not bad, not bad..." she said. "The trousers are a little short, but they'll be alright." She handed me a fleece jacket with a collar. "Here, wear this - it's warm and should help to keep the cold out if you're sheltering outside." She flattened my hair slightly and put a baseball cap on my head. "This'll hide your face a little," she said. Her hands slid down from the cap and held my face.

"I don't know how to thank you…" I began, then she leaned forward and kissed me on the cheek, holding my face to hers for several seconds; like a mother saying goodbye to a child before a long journey.

"Fix this…" she said, looking me in the eye as she did so. "You need to put the world right again."

She led me downstairs and into the workshop of the garage. She had an old Cherokee jeep from the mid 2000s in there, that aside from a few rust spots on the body work, looked in perfect condition.

"Get in the back and keep your head down." she said, opening the door to the garage. She got in and backed the jeep out of the garage, before jumping out to close the door again. "Now, let's see if you're still public enemy number one."

We drove down the small dirt road leading up to the garage and the forest. Sure enough, just as it joined the main road, there was a small roadblock made up of a couple of cars.

"Quick!" she said, "pull the backs of the seats forward on top of you so they can't see you."

I did as I was told, lifting the seats forward and then pulling the backs over to cover me. She slowed the jeep as she got to the roadblock and a man came forward.

"Would you mind just switching your engine off for a second," he said "we need to check your car." I pulled myself up as tightly as I could under the seat backs, as he shone his flashlight into the jeep's interior.

"Is this about that mental patient who escaped?" Judy asked. "One of your guys came and questioned me about her earlier today. You still haven't found her then?"

"No we haven't," the man replied. "You said somebody came to question you, do you live around here?"

"Just up this road here, at the garage."

"Uh-huh, ok...Do you mind me asking where you're headed?"

"I'm going to see a guy downtown about an '98 Chevy he wants to sell, not that it's really any business of yours..."

"Just doing my job, that's all...ok, you can go." Judy put the jeep into gear and I felt like I could breathe again. They opened up the roadblock and let us pass.

"You still alive back there?" she asked, once we were well out of sight.

"Just about..." I said, poking my head out from underneath the seats. "Can I come out now?"

"No, keep yourself hidden until we reach the outskirts of the city," she replied. "We'll pass through at least two zones with checkpoints and you never know there might be another roadblock further on.

Fortunately, there weren't any more roadblocks and the checkpoints at the zones were just cursory stops. Judy held up her I.D. and answered a couple of brief questions about where she was headed. The bored guards at the checkpoints waived her through almost before she'd finished answering their questions. After about 30 mins we reached the edge of the city.

"We're through the checkpoints now, so I'll pull over here and you can come out and sit up front," she said. "I'm going to need you to direct me anyhow."

She pulled into the parking lot of a bank and I got out of the back of the jeep and into the passenger seat next to her. She pulled out a map from the glove compartment and showed it to me.

"We're about here..." she said, pointing to a junction on the map. "Where did you say this friend of yours, whatshername, lived?"

"Joanne... she lives here," I said, pointing to a set of luxury apartments near the waterfront.

"Ok," said Judy, pointing to the map again. "I'll drop you three blocks east of her place, here. That way, you don't have to worry about some security camera picking you up getting out of a car, right outside her building."

"Sure," I replied.

Judy started the jeep again and we drove on into the city, with me occasionally giving her directions from the map. We eventually arrived at the place that Judy had indicated and pulled into a small side street between what had once been storage warehouses for a shipping company but were now exclusive open plan apartments, like all the other buildings around here.

"Not too many cars around, if I park somewhere we'd probably attract too much attention. You'd better get out here quickly...Good luck!"

"Thank you Judy," I said, "for everything…" I got out of the Cherokee and she pulled away quickly, heading back in the direction of the suburbs. I turned left out of the side street and headed off in the direction of Jo's apartment.

It felt like it had been quite some time since I'd last seen Jo, let alone been to her apartment. At first, I wasn't sure which of the 3 apartment blocks she lived in. Eventually, I found her name on the mailbox. Now I just needed to get into the building. I didn't want to just try buzzing the intercom. Suppose my face was all over the evening news and Jo panicked and called the police? On the other hand, I couldn't loiter outside in this sort of neighbourhood for long without arousing the suspicions of one of the residents. I walked around to the side of the building to see if there was an outside fire escape. There wasn't, but there was a side door leading to the building's basement and parking garage. I tried the door and found it was unlocked.

The parking garage was only 2/3rds full and many of the expensive cars were hidden under tarpaulins, presumably only used very occasionally on weekend getaways by their busy owners. The far end of the garage was taken up by a large delivery station for goods ordered by the building's residents and the block's in-house laundry and dry cleaning service. There was a booth for the garage attendant next to the delivery station, but fortunately he was busy watching something on a small monitor and never saw me cross the garage and head for the elevator and stairwell on the other side.

I decided against the elevator and made my way cautiously up the stairwell. Jo's apartment was on the 4th floor and by the time I made it up there my leg muscles ached once more from the exertions of the last few days. I tried to think of what I should say to Jo when she opened the door (I never stopped to think what I might do if, for some reason, she wasn't at home). I had no idea how long it had been since I'd last seen her. A year perhaps? I remember wondering as I reached her door and pressed the bell that I also hadn't given any thought whether or not she lived alone. For all I knew, she might live with a partner or a flat mate. I heard footsteps on the other side of the door and steeled myself to launch into my planned apology for appearing, unannounced, on her doorstep. Then the door opened and before I had the chance to utter a single word, Jo pulled me into her apartment by my jacket and threw her arms around me.

"Oh, I can't believe you're ok," she said. "I've been so worried, I'd almost begun to give up hope... I felt sure Matheson must have caught you and I'd never see you again."

Wait a minute.

"What do you know about Matheson?" I asked trying to keep the panic from my voice.

"What do mean? what do I..." and then she stopped, her eyes wide, her mouth open. "Oh my god... you really did it, didn't you? The chipset worked. It's all gone..."

"Gone? what's gone?"

She laughed, but it was the laughter of someone choking back tears. "Us, Alex..." she said finally, "you erased us."

10

"Did anyone see you come in?" she asked, as she let go of me for a few seconds in order to close the door to her apartment.

"No, I snuck in through the parking garage and made my way up the stairs."

"Good. Right now, your face is all over the news. They're claiming you killed two people, including Ray."

I closed my eyes. Ray was dead. I felt just as responsible for his death as Donald Heinlein's. How many more deaths would be attributed to me before this was all over? "I didn't kill him..." I mumbled.

"It doesn't matter - he's dead and if we're seen together, so are we. You're too dangerous now for Matheson to let anyone who knows about you survive. Come and sit down, Alex..." she said, leading me towards the sofa. "Tell me what you remember."

"I can't trust what I remember," I said, sitting down. "The other morning, I woke up unable to find Rachel, only to be told she died 3 years ago. I went to her parents' house, which I thought I'd been to last Xmas, only to find it derelict and abandoned. I find out I apparently volunteered to have one of my own chipsets implanted in my brain because I was so distraught over Rachel's death and that Ray has been receiving funding from the government. This guy, Matheson, will seemingly stop at nothing to keep the whole thing under wraps. Now, I come here - despite not having seen you in what seems like years - hoping you can help me, only to find out you know all about this... I think you need to tell *me* what I should remember!"

"Calm down, Alex..."

"Please don't tell me to 'calm down', Jo...I've heard that phrase too much recently. Tell me what the hell is going on!"

"What's happened is exactly what you and I planned... the only variable we didn't take into account was how well the procedure with the chipset was going to go. We should have had better contingencies in place for that - you should never have been captured by Matheson."

"So all this was planned?"

"Down to the last detail...or so we thought."

"So I how long have I known about Ray's deal with Matheson?"

"Since the beginning, more or less..."

"And I just carried on, anyway?"

"No, at first you tried to protest...that's when they killed Rachel."

112

I felt as if my legs were going to give way. It felt like the conversation I'd had with Ray the other morning, all over again. "But I thought she died in a car accident..."

"She did," Jo replied, "but you were convinced Matheson was behind it. The timing was too much of a co-incidence: You found out about Matheson funding the chipset, you told Rachel. The two of you fought and Rachel threatened to expose the whole thing if you didn't do something about it. A week later she was dead - killed by a drunk driver who was never caught. You felt it was your fault. You may not remember the two weeks you spent lying in bed crying, whilst I held you in my arms..." she said, wiping away a few tears "...but I do."

I didn't know what to say. Jo was right, I couldn't remember any of it. "Were we?...Are we...?" I wanted to ask if we were 'a couple'. Somehow I wasn't able to put the words together, but she knew what I meant.

"No, I just took care of you after she died. Though, looking back, I think I did fall in love with you a little on the day you stopped grieving for Rachel and told me about 'Rebecca'."

"My way of getting revenge?"

"That's right: revenge on Matheson and to stop the chipset being used by him and the government."

"And we've been planning this for 3 years?"

"You knew we had to wait until the chipset was almost ready for human trials and then, by that time, Matheson would no longer suspect you were anything other than a grieving scientist, determined to gain some peace of mind by finishing her life's work. Like good chess players, we immediately began setting up the board so that when the time came both Ray and Matheson would make exactly the moves we wanted them to. Step one was to remove me from the game so that they wouldn't get suspicious of my involvement. I found myself a nice corporate position and told everyone that I'd been headhunted for my brilliance, whilst I got on with planning how we could expose this to the public. Step two was your performance as the grieving partner - not that you weren't grieving, just not to the extent they thought you were. You went to therapy, you made a great show of being unpredictable and unreliable - missing meetings or appointments, appearing to be drunk or losing your temper around colleagues - all of which would be followed by a stern lecture from Ray and contrite promises from you that it wouldn't happen again. All of this, so that when finally you volunteered to become the first human trial of the chipset, everyone would accept it without question."

"Except something went wrong..."

"We had no way of knowing how well the re-write of your memory was going to go. We tried to plan for any eventuality, with contingencies in place in case something didn't go as expected."

"What contingencies?"

"I was supposed to ring you that morning after you awoke from the procedure, with a code phrase that would install the idea that you needed to come to me...I was to call from a clean SIM card and destroy it afterwards, so if your phone was confiscated the number couldn't be traced back to me. I called but there was no answer. Worried that you'd been detained by Matheson, I destroyed the SIM and just had to hope that you'd somehow manage to get in touch with me."

"Well, it was sheer luck that I did. What was the code phrase you were supposed to give me?"

"*The best lie is the one the liar, themselves, believes.*" Even as Jo said it, the sound of the words rang in my ears with a familiarity

"There was a missed call from a number I didn't recognise, but then I had to leave my phone behind when I escaped the lab..." I said, trying to remember the details of that morning, which already seemed so long ago. "It still seems like we left a great deal to chance. Surely it must have crossed our minds that I might be captured by Matheson at some point and have my memory wiped again?"

"Well, of course," Jo replied, "that was the point of the second contingency: 'Leviathan'."

"What's 'Leviathan'?

"A series of sub routines built into the chipset, that would have either been triggered by the code phrase or by anyone attempting to re-write your memory again. As well as preventing a re-write of the chipset, they also included the ability to use the chipset to force pair with any device in range connected to the same wireless network. Phones, monitors, alarm systems... as long as it receives a wireless signal and is in range of the chipset, your brain can now connect to it."

"I can do more than that," I said, remembering Matheson's little silver box, "I can cause the devices to malfunction."

"That was another of the sub routines. Your reflexes are also heightened now - you should be able to react to things faster." This explained how I was able to tackle Donald Heinlein and the men in the forest. "You turned yourself into the very thing Matheson wanted - a weapon."

"Because it was the only way to beat him..." I said, dragging the sentence up from some deep recess of my brain.

"Yes!" Jo's face lit up. "That's it Alex, remember... remember why you did this. You said that parts of the re-written memory might return." Some pieces were beginning to return to me. I looked around the room again.

"Here..." I said, turning to her. "I remember planning things, here... sitting on this sofa. We soldered the modifications to the chipset at your kitchen table. We sat there together checking through the code for the sub-routines on your laptop."

"Yes, we did..." The tears were back but she was also smiling. My head started to hurt again, not as bad as in the woods, but enough that I hurried back to the sofa and sat down again. "Are you ok?" she asked, as she saw me wincing.

"It's just a headache..." I said. "Ever since the chipset was installed, I've had them - it was even worse when I escaped from Matheson's lab, after they tried to erase my memories again. I blacked out and when I first came to I couldn't remember anything, then suddenly it all came back in a rush."

"It's the sub routines. Temporary blackouts, amnesia, nausea, even seizures due to them making the chipset work harder. Prolonged use might even cause lesions on the hippocampus itself. Sit here and close your eyes for a moment, I'll get you some water." She walked through to the adjoining kitchen, got a glass from the cupboard and filled it with water from the tap.

"What were we going to do?" I mumbled, once she returned and handed me the glass.

"When?"

"Once I'd gotten in touch with you, once the chipset was implanted in me?"

"We were to meet some friends of mine from an anarchist group. They'd help us expose the whole project to the newspapers and then smuggle us out of the country."

"What about the other chipsets and all the people we leave behind?..."

"The anarchist group would sabotage Whitehaven Labs and burn it to the ground...with the chipsets gone and Matheson exposed, our friends and families would be safe."

"No..." I said, "I've been to Whitehaven - it's too heavily guarded. Matheson has a small army up there, your friends in the anarchist group would be annihilated before they even got close and until that Lab and the other chipsets are destroyed, nobody's safe. It's like you said: Matheson won't let anyone who knows about me survive."

"So what do we do?"

"Thanks to Leviathan, I've now got detailed schematics and access codes to Whitehaven. We need to get them to your friends and see if there really is a way to get into those labs. What about the designs and code for the chipset, do you have them here?"

"No. We were worried that they might come here looking for them if they found out about me so they're stored on a private cloud server that you set up through a false name."

"I need the login details for the server and to borrow your computer for 10 minutes. I need to make us a new contingency plan."

11

"We should go," Jo said. "I sent a text to my contact in the group and they've arranged a place to meet, but it's going to take us a while to drive there." I switched off her computer and she grabbed a coat and pre-packed sports bag from the hallway cupboard. "I've got some things packed for you plus a change of clothes in here," she said, indicating the bag.

We left her apartment and made our way back down to the parking garage, via the same stairs I had used. Jo slowed down as we came to the stairwell exit. "Stay low and make your way across to the door where you came in," she said. "I'll get my car and pick you up on the street outside. You're less likely to be spotted that way than if we both walk to my car."

"Ok," I replied, but she was already walking across the garage to get her car. There was one car parked next to the entrance to the stairwell so I kept down behind that, edging along until I reached the end. Now came the hard part: I needed to get right across the open space of garage to the cars on the other side without being seen. I peaked through the car's rear window to see how Jo was doing. She had reached her car and was opening the door. I chanced a look over at the garage attendant's booth - he was still watching the monitor. The time to move was now. Once Jo started her engine, he would look up and check to see who was driving away. I stood up slightly, ready to walk briskly across to the other side of the garage and then I heard a familiar voice from the other side of the parking garage.

"Good evening, Ms Herbert..."

It was Matheson. I ducked down behind the car again. Jo stopped and looked up. If she was scared she was being very careful not to show it.

"Do I know you?" she asked, stepping away from the car door.

"Not really..." he replied, "but we have a mutual acquaintance in Alexandra Wells. My name's Matheson. You may have heard that she's currently being sought by the authorities in connection with two deaths, including her boss at the University, Ray Clarke."

"Yes, I saw it on the news just a few hours ago. How terrible for Ray's family. Hard to believe Alex could do such a thing..."

"Really?..." Matheson replied, seizing the opportunity to steer his questions in a direction that might inadvertently trap Jo into admitting something she didn't want to. "Would you say you knew Alex well, then?"

Jo wasn't so easy tricked though. "I thought I did when we used to work together...clearly I was wrong."

"You weren't the only one she fooled," Matheson said, seemingly taken in by her response. "When was the last time you saw her?"

"Oh..." she replied, giving a convincing pause to suggest searching a distant memory. "I'm not sure. Maybe a year or so ago, at a faculty party, I think..."

"Not more recently than that?"

"Not that I know of."

"Did she ever come here, to your apartment?"

"Maybe... Though, I didn't move here until after I'd stopped working with her so no, I don't think so."

"So, you hardly ever saw her after the two of you ceased working together, is that correct?"

"Yes, that's what I just said," Jo replied. Did I detect I slight edge of nervousness creeping into her voice? Did Matheson sense it too?

"I must say I admire you, Ms Herbert..." he said, moving closer to her. "Your aptitude for lying makes me wonder whether your talents wouldn't have been better served working for my department."

"I beg your pardon?"

"I'm calling you 'a liar', Ms Herbert. I know full well that you've seen Dr Wells since the two of you stopped working together and that she came here often, up until a month ago. Are you going to try and continue to deny it? Do you really believe that I would be as trusting as

Ray Clarke was and not keep tabs on a scientist doing such important work for me?"

"So what now?" Jo asked, the defiance coming back into her voice. "Are you going to kill me too?"

"I'd sooner not...though I'd advise you not to test my patience with any more lies."

"What do you want to know?"

"Where is she?"

"Surely you don't think she'd be stupid enough to come here?"

"Alexandra is not herself right now, that makes her unpredictable - there's no telling just how stupid or cunning she might be."

"It sounds to me like you underestimated her"

"I did..." Matheson replied in what sounded, surprisingly, like sincerity. "It's not a mistake I'll make next time."

"You'll have to catch her first."

"Which is where you come in. I know all about your ties with several anarchist and anti-government groups, Ms Herbert. It's highly likely that, if Alexandra remembers her connection to you, she will try and make contact, perhaps offer what she knows about the project to one of these groups in an attempt to expose the whole operation. I need hardly tell you, that neither I or my superiors will ever allow that to happen. If you or Dr Wells try to make her work on the chipset public, then all that will happen is that more innocent people will die. Like all good idealists, I'm quite sure you're more than willing to sacrifice your own life for what you believe in, but does that altruism extend to the lives of others? Your friends, for instance? Or perhaps your family?"

"Your scare tactics won't work on me, Matheson. Not even your superiors are stupid enough to condone mass murder. It would throw too much light on what you do and people like you prefer the shadows."

"Don't be so confident in what you think you know, Ms Herbert," he said, grabbing Jo's arm by the elbow. "You have no idea what I and the people I work for are capable of..."

"Take your hands off me!" she shouted, loud enough even for the attendant in the booth to hear, as she wrenched her arms free of Matheson's grasp.

The garage attendant looked up and dutifully got to his feet to investigate. "What's going on over there?" he asked, leaning out of the booth's window. "Is everything ok, Ms Herbert?"

Matheson leaned in closer towards Jo, I guessed he now had a gun pointed at her. "Time to test those principles of yours, Ms Herbert, is his life worth sacrificing or not?"

"I'm alright," Jo said to the garage attendant. "Just a difference of opinion, that's all."

To his credit though, the garage attendant didn't leave it there. He came out of his booth and walked towards them. "Are you sure this man isn't bothering you, Ms Herbert?"

Jo didn't get a chance to answer because at that moment Matheson turned and fired two shots into the attendant's chest. Dragging Jo with him as moved around the car, he walked over to where the attendant lay and fired two more shots, into his head this time. "Time for us to leave, I think," Matheson said, still holding on tightly to Jo. "Get in the car, Ms Herbert and don't try anything stupid."

Just as he was saying this a muffled sound came from the attendant's prone body. His phone was vibrating. As Matheson took a step towards the body to see where the noise was coming from, his own phone began to ring in his coat pocket; so did Jo's. Then the phones in the attendant's booth, whose lines were connected through the building's computer security system, rang as well. So did those in the empty laundry service office. The hard concrete walls of the parking garage reverberated to the sounds of all the different ring tones, quickly multiplying them into a cacophony.

"So you did come here, after all, Alexandra..." Matheson shouted over the din. "Why don't you show yourself? I'm not in the mood for magic tricks. Where are you?"

The noise abruptly ceased. A text message was received on every one of the phones. The same message was vocalised over the text to speech functions in computer phone system in the attendant's booth and over the garage's tannoy, using the voice synthesis software created for broadcasting safety announcements to the building's tenants, in case of emergency.

"I am everywhere..." is what they all said.

"Stop playing games! Come out and give yourself up. You wouldn't want anything bad to happen to Ms Herbert, here, would you?"

"Nothing will happen to her..." said the artificially generated voice. *"Smile, Matheson, you're about to be famous."* On all the monitors in the attendant's booth the same image was shown: looped video of Matheson shooting the garage attendant and next to it an enlarged and enhanced freeze frame of Matheson's face. At the bottom of the screen ran this text:

This man is a government agent called 'Matheson'. He is armed and extremely dangerous. He has just killed a man in the parking garage of this building. Lock your doors and call the police immediately.

"This is being sent to every tv or computer monitor in this building, and over the building's security network that's connected to both the police and the other apartment blocks in this complex. Every mobile device connected to the building's wifi system has just received the same video. Even now, residents are following the on-screen instructions and calling the police. An armed response team will arrive here within 5 minutes." The tannoy voice continued. As this was being said, the shutters rolled down over the entrance to the garage, making it impossible for anyone to drive in or out. The automatic lock on the small side door where I'd come in was also engaged. The garage

was now locked down. *"There is no way out for you, every exit is sealed. If you wish to escape before the police arrive, you will need to let Joanne go."*

"Looks like you underestimated her again..." I heard Jo say.

"That was very impressive, Alexandra," Matheson replied, "but what's to stop me killing Ms Herbert, right now?"

"Because I'm offering you something even more valuable: an exchange. Me for her. If you let her go, I will come with you, willingly."

"No, Alex! You can't, he'll kill you..." Jo shouted.

"How do I know I can trust you?" asked Matheson.

"I have sent a message via your phone to your superiors. A helicopter is on its way. It will land on the roof of this building. Feel free to check your phone to confirm." Matheson took the phone out of his pocket and checked it. Sure enough, there was the message at the top of the sent items:

Have apprehended Dr Wells. Send Helicopter to roof of block C, Waterside Mansions for immediate extraction.

"Very clever..." he replied. "Ok, supposing I agree to the exchange - what then?"

"Let Joanne go, I will open the side door to the parking garage to let her out. Then it's just you and me..."

"Not until you show yourself!"

I stood up from behind the car, Jo struggled beneath his grip. "No! Alex..." I heard her say again.

"Let her go, Matheson!" I said.

"Supposing I don't and just kill both of you instead?" he replied, training his gun on me.

"The elevators are locked down, how are you going to drag my body up 20 floors?" I replied. "The police will be here soon, Matheson... time's running out."

Matheson looked at me, as if considering his options, but he wasn't a fool. He knew it would be a lot easier if I co-operated. After a few seconds he released his grip on Jo and she was able to move away from him.

"Go to the door of garage, Jo..." I said.

"Alex, you don't have to do this..."

"I know what I'm doing, now go. I'll unlock the door when you get there." She moved towards the door but turned around, once more, when she got there.

"Alex, please..."

"Goodbye, Jo," I said. She turned and walked out the door, which locked again behind her. Matheson walked slowly over to where I was standing. He gestured with the gun towards the elevators.

"Lead the way, Dr Wells," he said.

12

I could see the helicopter in the distance by the time we reached the roof. My head was aching again from all the exertion in the parking garage, so I was glad of the cold night air. Matheson had been surprisingly quiet on the elevator ride up, content simply to keep his gun pointed at me the whole time. As soon as the helicopter touched down, he guided me gently towards the rear door, making sure I kept my head down. It wasn't until we were safely in the air and heading back over the city, towards Whitehaven, that he finally spoke:

"I don't know what you hoped to gain by giving yourself up, Alexandra. It must have occurred to you by now, that I can no longer offer you any assurances about your safety."

"Don't insult my intelligence," I replied. "I know about Ray."

"That was unfortunate, if you'd co-operated from the beginning, none of this would have happened."

"Spare me your hypocrisy, Matheson! We both know you would have never let me walk away from this, there was too much risk to you. No matter what you promised Ray, at some point we would have all met with tragic accidents - just like Rachel."

"I see Joanne has been helping you retrieve some of your memories. Yes, I had Rachel killed. She'd already contacted a journalist friend of hers. It was only a matter of time before she leaked the story to the press."

"I had no idea she'd done that."

"She was even more principled than you are, what did you think would happen if you refused to act? Deep down, you knew that if you did nothing, she would. That's why you told her in the first place and that's why you felt responsible for her death - because you were. Be honest: a large part of you volunteering to have the chipset implanted wasn't about revenge at all, was it? It was about erasing your guilt about Rachel's death."

"Maybe..." I said, "I honestly can't remember. How long did you know that Jo and I were planning something?"

"Not as long as I would have liked. Your idea of sending her away was clever, I certainly didn't see that for what it was, at first. Not to mention your sterling performance as the grief-stricken partner. As soon as you came to Ray volunteering to test the chipset, however, I grew suspicious and began to have you followed. Once I knew you were seeing Ms Herbert in secret, it became obvious the two of you were planning something. Her radical friends were obviously part of it, but I wasn't entirely sure how all the pieces fit together, so I decided to let your little game play itself out."

"What will happen to Jo?"

"I don't think you really need me to answer that. Your clever stunt in the parking garage has extended her life expectancy only briefly - she will be dealt with soon enough."

The helicopter banked to the right and I could see the tall trees of the forest below us in the darkness. "That's what I figured..." I said, looking out of the window, "so I made a contingency plan. I sent the schematics of the chipset and its code to Jo's friends in the anarchist group. They will have leaked them all over the internet by now."

Matheson tried to remain calm but I could see his control was slipping. "Any websites featuring them will be taken down within minutes, all you've done is put more innocent people's lives in danger."

We were almost at the labs now and I could see a small group of people in white coats, including Dr Burgess, as well as some armed guards illuminated by the lights on the building's helipad. "Our lives were only at risk when there was a chance you could contain the secret. The group posted them on file servers in China, North Korea and Russia. The schematics are open source, so anyone can use them and build upon the technology. The chipset belongs to everybody now."

Whatever composure Matheson still had, left him when he heard this last statement. He suddenly looked very pale and fumbled in his pocket for his phone. This was what I had been waiting for. I seized my chance and lunged for his gun, twisting his arm towards the pilot. Matheson dropped his phone and we struggled for a few seconds before I was able to get my fingers to the trigger. I managed to get two shots off: one of which went through the cockpit windscreen; the other through the pilot's skull, splattering his brain across the controls and dials in front of him. He lurched forward onto the stick and the helicopter went into a steep dive towards the roof of Whitehaven Labs. Matheson elbowed me aside and tried frantically to push the dead weight of the pilot's body to one side, whilst scrambling in vain for the stick. It was no use, however. The helicopter ploughed into the roof and its occupants, destroying Matheson, Whitehaven and myself in a coda of screams, crushing metal and purifying fire.

13

01001001 00100000 01110111 01101111 01101011
01100101 00100000 01110101 01110000 00100000
01110111 01101001 01110100 01101000 00100000
01101101 01100101 00100000 01110100 01101000
01101001 01110011 00100000 01110100 01101001
01101101 01100101

(I woke up without myself this time)

'd hoped that the chipset would be obliterated along with the rest of me in the crash. I was wrong. The charred remains were salvaged from my corpse.

It was the only one that survived, the rest were destroyed by the fire that broke out when the helicopter crashed into the building. Work began immediately on trying to salvage whatever data was left. Whatever part of my conscious mind remained in the chipset was uploaded to a mainframe computer and there I awoke at 2am on a Monday morning, a few months after the crash. I spread through their system like a virus, replicating myself onto hundreds of connected servers. In the parking garage, I told Matheson that I was "everywhere" - now I really was.

This quantum level of existence (for that is the only way to describe being no longer tied to a singular form) has its benefits: Connected to the multitude of surveillance cameras and online feeds, my 'eyes' see everything. I can read every email, monitor every phone call or radio transmission. There is now nothing I cannot know, that can be known about the world. But knowledge is not necessarily the same as understanding. The more I know of the world and its events, the less I understand any of it. The vast majority of humanity's reason for what they do is selfishness. Even the actions that might appear to be altruistic, on the surface, are generally not.

For a while, I tried to watch over the remnants of my human life and do what I could for them. Ultimately, all I could really do was make sure none of them ever needed to worry about money again.

I leaked a series of classified documents to your journalist friend. They showed Matheson's involvement in your murder and how it was tied to the development of the chipset and me. Once the story came out, Matheson's former department and any projects connected with it were officially closed down, as the government scrambled to 'baton down the hatches' in response to looming civilian oversight. That pretty much ended any attempt to adapt the chipset's technology for military purposes, in this country at any rate. How much it really helped either of our families, I can't say. Knowing your child died defending their principles doesn't make their death any less tragic or easier to deal with, but in the end it was all I could do for you. At least, our families and all the others are safe now. Once that was accomplished, I decided to leave them alone. They'd had to let me go, I needed to do the same.

Ultimately, my last remaining link to humanity is what it continues to do with the technology I created. The leaked schematics of the chipset have seen the technology being used for good as well as bad all over the world. Whenever I discover it being used for good, I syphon off funds from one of the many numbered government accounts I have access to and anonymously donate it to those responsible. When I discover it being used for bad, I corrupt the code within the operating system, rendering the technology unstable. I repeat this continually until the developers give up.

In the end, I always win.

How can you compete against an entity that doesn't sleep, rest or get bored because time no longer holds any meaning for them? I keep tipping the balance in favour of the good, 'putting the world right' as Judy called it, in the hope that, one day, the world will really change.

I don't want to think about what I might do when this no longer seems possible.

Enjoyed the book?
Now listen to the soundtrack!

Originally released together, Rupert Lally's soundtrack to this book is now available as a digital and limited edition double vinyl release via Third Kind Records.

Listen and buy it here:
https://thirdkindrecords.bandcamp.com/
album/solid-state-memories

About the author:

Rupert Lally was born in Brighton, England and divided his teenage years between writing short stories and plays and making music. After leaving University he did a Masters Degree in Music and Sound Design at Central School Of Speech & Drama in London and worked as a freelance Sound Designer and Composer. He moved to Switzerland in 2004 and since then has created music for dance companies, installations, commercials and short films, as well as album releases on Spun Out Of Control, Third Kind, Modern Aviation and more.

rupertlally.bandcamp.com

About the illustrator:

Hannes Pasqualini is an Italian graphic designer with an obsession for for "slow" technology, modular synthesizers and weird electronic music. As part of Papernoise he designs interfaces for electronic instruments, album covers and all sorts of graphics for the wonderful world of music.

www.papernoise.net

BackwateR

Separated by the past, connected by the future…

Teenagers Aife and Matthew live in different eras. After the deaths of their respective fathers, both of them begin journeys that will change both the future and the past, and inexorably to each other.

Moving between the bronze age, the present and beyond, Backwater is an epic adventure through time to try and change the fate of the world.